BIG PICTURE

Other Books by
PERCIVAL EVERETT

BIG PICTURE

Stories by

PERCIVAL EVERETT

GRAYWOLF PRESS

Publication of this volume is made possible in part by a grant provided by the Minnesota State Arts Board through an appropriation by the Minnesota State Legislature, and by a grant from the National Endowment for the Arts. Significant additional support has been provided by the Andrew W. Mellon Foundation, the Lila Wallace–Reader's Digest Fund, the McKnight Foundation, and other generous contributions from foundations, corporations, and individuals. Graywolf Press is a member agency of United Arts, Saint Paul. To these organizations and individuals who make our work possible, we offer heartfelt thanks.

Published by Graywolf Press
2402 University Avenue, Suite 203
Saint Paul, Minnesota 55114
All rights reserved.

Printed in the United States of America.

ISBN 1-55597-238-1

2 4 6 8 9 7 5 3 1
First Graywolf Printing, 1996

Library of Congress Catalog Card Number: 95-80897

Acknowledgments

The author wishes to express his gratitude to the editors of the following publications in which the stories below first appeared.

"Squeeze" was first published in *Callaloo,* Vol. 16, No. 3, 1993. "Throwing Earth" was first published in the *Texas Review,* Vol. XI, Nos. 3 & 4, 1990; and also in *That's What I Like About the South: Southern Short Fiction for the 1990s*, Eds. George Garrett and Paul Ruffin, University of South Carolina Press, 1993. "Turned Out" (under the title "Bull Does Nothing") was first published in *Callaloo*, Vol. 12, No. 1, 1989.

Contents

For Candida, whose first concern is always the work

Cerulean

The front left wheel of the lawn mower looked like it was ready to fall off. The machine's original blue was now rust red and brown and the writing on it that at one time had read WESTERN AUTO now said TERN AU. The wheel wobbled with a rhythmic squeak as the short man with the shaved spot on his head pushed the mower up the walk toward Gail and Michael. They were standing at their door, bags of groceries at their feet while Michael dug into his pockets for his keys. The man with the mower stopped at the bottom of the steps and looked up at them.

Michael looked at the man, then at Gail, then at his grass, which didn't appear to be in great need of cutting.

The man raised five fingers and pointed to the yard.

"Five dollars?" Michael asked.

The man nodded, then rubbed his nose while he looked away.

Michael turned to Gail, who shrugged. Michael studied the man's filthy jeans and his shirt, which appeared to be made of a fabric too heavy for the heat. "Okay," he said. "Five bucks."

The man didn't say anything. He turned and walked to the edge of the yard and started pulling the cord of his machine's little motor.

Michael found his keys and got the door open. Inside, he and Gail set the sacks on the counter.

"Are you sure that was a good idea?" Gail asked, putting the milk into the refrigerator.

"It's five dollars," Michael said.

"I don't mean the money."

1

Michael sat at the table and watched as Gail put away a few things. "I think it's okay." He paused to listen to the motor outside. "The grass doesn't really need to be mowed, so what can he mess up?"

"I don't mean that either," Gail said. She opened a new bottle of cranberry juice and poured a glass. "What if he sees us as a soft touch?"

"We are a soft touch." Michael stood and walked to the window. "It must be ninety degrees out there and he's wearing a wool shirt."

"He can take it off if he wants," Gail said.

"Well, he's not doing it. He's sweating like crazy out there. What if he has a heat stroke while he's working for us?" Michael considered that.

"What is it?" Gail asked.

"I'm going to give him one of my T-shirts." He went upstairs and into their bedroom. He pulled a light blue shirt from the shelf in the closet. The letters UNC were faded. He took the shirt back to the kitchen. Gail was still putting food away.

"You're not serious," she said.

"If he keels over, we could be liable."

Gail paused. "I suppose."

"I'm going to ask him to change into this." The sun was slicing into his back as Michael walked out the back door and across the yard toward the man. He waved to him when a few yards away. The man stopped pushing the mower and watched Michael approach. He didn't turn off the machine. "I brought you this shirt," Michael said loudly.

The man looked at it, but didn't seem to understand.

Michael pointed to the man's soaked wool garment and then held the T-shirt out to him. The man nodded and unbuttoned what he was wearing. He took it off, handed it to Michael, and took the T-shirt. The wool was indeed soaked and Michael felt uncomfortable holding it. The man pulled the light blue shirt over his head, his hair wet from perspiration, and down over his soft, glistening belly. He nodded a thank you and went back to pushing the machine. Michael walked back to the house, and draped the wet shirt over the railing of the steps. Inside, he walked to the sink and washed his hands.

Gail was peering out the window over the sink. "I see he put it on."

Michael dried his hands with a couple of paper towels. "Yeah. He was sweating like a pig. It's unbelievable out there."

"He asked to do it," Gail said. "Do you think he can't talk?"

Michael shrugged. "You know, that's a big job for only five dollars."

"He's the one who asked for it," Gail said.

"Yeah, but it's sweltering out there. It'll take him a couple of hours. He'll use a buck's worth of gas at least. So, he's doing it for four dollars."

"Have you ever heard the term 'bleeding heart?'"

"Tell me it doesn't bother you," Michael said.

"Of course it bothers me." Gail sat at the table with him. "But I am glad you didn't bring that shirt in here."

"That's something else that bothered me." Michael leaned his head back and blew out a breath. "I was really uncomfortable handling that thing after he'd been wearing it."

"Who wouldn't be?" Gail laughed. "It's soaked with sweat and who knows what else."

"I know, but still . . ."

A couple of hours went by and there was a knock at the door. Michael found the man standing there, his lawn mower at the bottom of the steps. He had his wool shirt back on, but it was not buttoned. His chest hair was shining with sweat and moisture sat in the cracks of his belly. He held the blue T-shirt by his side.

"All done?" Michael asked.

The man nodded.

Michael put his hand in his pocket. "Do you live around here?"

Another nod.

"Which way?"

He pointed up the streeet toward the busy avenue.

Michael handed the man his money. "Here's ten dollars. It was a bigger job than I thought at first."

The man looked at the ten, then fished a five out of his pocket and pushed it toward Michael.

"No, it's all for you," Michael said.

But the man shoved the five at him again. Michael felt obliged to take it and did. The man then handed Michael the sweaty, light blue T-shirt. Michael took it, and his fingers touched the slick, salty water from the man's body. He closed his hand around it and looked at the yard.

"You did a fine job. Thank you."

The man stepped back down the steps, grabbed the handle of his mower, and walked away up the street.

Michael closed the door and felt the air conditioner switch on and pump coolness at him from above. He went into the back room and put the UNC T-shirt on top of the washing machine. While he was standing at the kitchen sink lathering up his hands Gail came in.

"So, how much did you pay him?" she asked.

"Five dollars," he said, tearing off a couple of towels from the roll.

"I'm impressed."

"I tried to give him a ten, but he gave me change. Still didn't say a word."

"I wonder if he can hear," Gail said.

"Don't know."

"I'll bet he reads lips. And I'll bet that's how he can stand out there with that noisy machine for hours."

"Possibly."

"What's wrong?" Gail asked.

"Nothing." Michael opened the refrigerator and just stared inside. "It's really hot out there. You think he has a place to live?"

"Who knows," Gail said. "Hand me a diet cola."

Michael grabbed a can and gave it to her. Opening the can she cut her finger and shook it in the air. She took a swallow. "So, who's going to cook?" she asked.

"I will."

"That was easy. I'll help."

Later that night, after dinner, Gail was watching television and nursing another diet soda. She sat in the overstuffed chair with her legs folded under her. Michael passed through on his way to the bookshelf against the far wall.

"They're talking about the suicides at the Golden Gate Bridge," she said, referring to the program on the television. "This guy is supposedly an expert on suicide." She laughed. "How can you be an expert on suicide and still be alive?"

Michael chuckled, too. "I suppose that's a good point."

"What are you doing?" she asked.

"I thought I'd sit in the other room and read for a while."

"Come on, sit in here with me and watch something stupid."

"Nah, I'm just going to read."

"Come on, veg with me."

Michael looked at the book in his hand.

"You can sit on the floor in front of me and I'll rub your neck."

Michael tossed the book onto the coffee table and sat in front of her. "You're a terrible influence."

"That's why you married me. Because I like to give."

"Does your mother know how you talk?"

"Nope."

Michael felt his wife's fingers on his neck and watched the images of the bridge in San Francisco. "Do you mind if we watch something else?"

Gail picked up the remote control and switched channels, moving past an old movie, a soccer game, a couple of ads, and settled on an exercise show. The woman leading the group counted out loud between whoops and encouraging words.

"You're not serious?" Michael said.

"Do you think she has a good body?" Gail asked.

"She ought to; she exercises for a living." He watched the woman in spandex. "Actually, I don't like her body. I don't like her legs."

"They're thin."

"So? What's thin got to do with anything? Her legs are shapeless." He turned and looked at Gail. "Now your legs . . . your legs are not shapeless." He pretended to bite her knee.

"Oh yeah?"

"Yeah." He puckered his lips. "Kiss me."

Gail leaned forward and kissed him. A noise in the backyard caused her to sit up straight. "What was that?"

"Don't know," Michael said.

"Do you love me?"

Michael reached and took his wife's hand. "Yes, I love you. You know I love you."

"There's that sound again," Gail said.

"I'll go see what it is," Michael said and found his feet. Gail followed him into the kitchen. They didn't turn on the lights. Michael looked out the door window and Gail looked out through the window over the sink. "I don't see anything." Michael opened the door and stepped out onto the small deck. He looked over at the garbage cans and saw that one of the metal lids was on the ground. He walked down and put the top back on the container, thought he heard something behind him, but turned and found nothing.

Gail called to Michael from the door.

"It must have a been a cat or a dog," he said. He pressed the lid firmly down and stepped back up to the door. "Yeah, cat or dog, maybe a bear or hyena."

"Or a duck-billed platypus."

Upstairs in bed, Michael felt the little movements that told him his wife was close. He tried to think of his love for her, but it seemed to get lost in his head. He felt her come, then shut his eyes and rested his face on her thigh.

The next morning Michael returned from his run and jumped into the shower. He kept the water cool. He was tired of the hot summer weather. He made the water a little colder and let it strike his face. His knees ached a bit and he remembered a time when they didn't, when his runs were longer and seemed less boring. He turned off the water, grabbed a towel from the rod, and dried. It was Sunday and he'd promised Gail that he would try to get the dryer to stop making a new, high-pitched whine. He slid open the closet door and there, sitting on top of a stack of sweaters and pullovers was the light blue UNC T-shirt. He stared at it. Gail must have washed it and run it through the whining dryer while he was out running. He touched it, thinking about how it had been on the body of that man. He was ashamed that he was afraid to put it on. He picked it up and sniffed it, found that it smelled like the soap they used. He tossed the shirt on the bed and looked at it while he found and put on underwear, socks, and a pair of jeans. He looked at himself in the mirror and noticed how old he was getting. He walked downstairs to the kitchen with the shirt in his hand. He took a yogurt from the refrigerator.

"I was wondering if you'd actually wear that shirt," Gail said. She had file folders open on the table and was making notes.

"What's the big deal? It's washed, right?"

Gail nodded. "I'm just surprised."

"Didn't mean to surprise you."

"Are you all right?" Gail asked.

"Sure. Why?"

"You didn't sleep well."

"No, I guess not." Michael rubbed his forehead.

"Are you happy?" she asked.

"It's just work, honey." He looked at her eyes. "I thought I'd look at the dryer," Michael said. "But I have no clue where that sound is coming from."

"Well, it drives me crazy. You know how those little high squeals can squirm all through the house and find you and get under your skin and make you want to kill the nearest person."

"I'll fix it." He slipped the shirt over his head and took a bite of yogurt.

"Good."

It was hot in the back room. The air conditioner failed to pump relief there and the morning sun pounded at the slatted windows. Michael had the dryer turned on its side and was checking the belt. The problem was, of course, that as long as the machine was disassembled it had to be unplugged, and therefore couldn't be turned on to allow him to hear the noise. The belt seemed tight enough without being too tight and all the screws and bolts were fast. He lay there on his back, reached inside, and sprayed the motor and belt with WD-40. He let his head fall back and stared at the ceiling. He scratched at his shoulder, then at his chest. Gail called to him from the kitchen.

"How's it coming?" she asked, now standing in the doorway.

Michael didn't say anything, just looked at her and shrugged. He started to put the dryer back together.

"You're soaked," Gail said.

Michael looked at himself and wiped the perspiration from his face.

"I'm going to make some lemonade."

He gave her the okay sign with his fingers and watched her turn away into the kitchen. Michael got the dryer back together and turned it on. It didn't whine. He didn't know why, but it sounded the way it was supposed to sound.

Gail leaned into the room. "All right, you fixed it," she said and was gone again.

Michael put away the tools. He felt good. He felt easy. He went back upstairs, stripped down, and got into the shower again. He put on another shirt and some shorts.

"Where's the lemonade?" he asked, walking into the kitchen.

"I'll pour you some," she said, opening the refrigerator.

Michael sat at the table and watched his wife. He loved the way she enjoyed her body, the way she moved. "Are you still working on the same chapter?" he asked her.

"I'm always working on the same chapter."

"That's not quite true."

"True enough," she said. She pushed a glass of lemonade in front of her husband.

"Thanks." Michael took a long swallow. It was cool and tasted good, but he felt a little out of sorts.

"It's really hot in the laundry room, eh?" Gail sat in front of her work at the table.

"Pretty warm."

"You looked sick out there. I'm glad you showered. You look a lot better now."

Michael nodded. "Wouldn't want to look sick."

There was a knock at the door and Michael got up and looked through the door window. It was the man from yesterday, with his lawn mower. "You're not going to believe this," he said to Gail.

"What?" Gail got up, came to the door, and looked out. "Didn't he finish the job?"

"I thought he had." Michael opened the door and stepped out into the heat.

The man pointed at the yard and held up five fingers again. Michael looked at the grass. Gail came out, too.

"You just mowed it all yesterday," Michael said.

The man flashed five fingers again.

"Thank you," Gail said, "but we don't need you today."

"I tried to give you ten dollars yesterday," Michael said. "Listen, I'll give you another five because you earned it, but we don't need our grass cut again." He turned to Gail. "Would you grab a five for me?"

Gail went back into the house.

"Can you talk?" Michael could smell the man, recognized the smell from when he had carried the wool shirt before. "Can you hear me or are you reading my lips?"

The man nodded and smiled.

Gail returned with the money. Michael took it from her and handed it to the man.

The man turned away and, somewhat relieved, Michael and Gail turned back into the house. Michael had just closed the door when the sound of the lawn mower split the air. He looked at Gail.

"That guy scares me," Gail said.

"He's harmless," Michael said.

"He's a nut."

Michael looked out the window at him, wearing the wool shirt, struggling to push his mower with the wobbly wheel. "He's pretty weird, all right. We'll let him do this today."

The man mowed the already mowed lawn and was gone without a knock at the door. Michael suddenly noticed the silence. He got up from his desk and walked from window to window, looking out.

"He's gone," he said to Gail.

"Good."

"Boy, that machine of his makes a lot of noise," Michael said. "Listen to how quiet it is now."

"Yep." Gail yawned and rubbed her eyes. "I hate work. I hate it. I hate it. I hate it."

"How old do you think that guy is?" Michael asked.

"If he comes back he won't get any older; that's all I know." Gail sharpened a pencil. "I don't know. Sixty?"

"I'd bet he's our age."

"Looks sixty."

"He does; you're right." Michael rubbed the back of his neck. "Of course, I feel sixty."

The following morning was overcast and Michael had trouble pulling himself out of bed for his run. Lately he'd had to force himself. He'd had to force work as well; the paintings were staring back at him, mocking him, scaring him. He tied the laces of his shoes and grabbed the nearest shirt, which happened to be the light blue UNC T-shirt. Gail stirred when he opened the door of the bedroom.

"Michael?"

"I'm going running," he said.

"Is it still dark?" she asked sleepily.

"No, just cloudy."

Her head fell back onto the pillow.

Michael walked down the stairs, pulling on the shirt. The morning was a bit cooler than it had been and Michael felt it helped him start at a better pace. He ran toward the avenue, crossed it, and turned up a street parallel to it. His strides felt good and long. Then he saw it. At the mouth of an alley, between a house and an old hardware store, was the wobbly wheeled lawn mower. It was parked next to the wall of the store. The store was dark and there was no one around. Michael slowed and then ran in place, staring at the mower. He looked at the house and wondered if the man lived there. He looked down the alley and saw that it opened onto the avenue. He ran that way and glanced around, not really knowing what he expected to see.

He arrived at home to find Gail collecting her papers at the table. "How was your run?"

Michael nodded and went to the cabinet for a glass and filled it with water from the bubbler.

"I'm going to make some breakfast," Gail said. "Would you like some?"

Michael shook his head.

"Are you okay?"

Michael blew out a breath and raised his water glass to her. Gail studied him for a second, then went back to her papers.

Michael set his glass on the counter and walked upstairs, pulling off his shirt on the way. He called back down to Gail, "Hey, I changed my mind."

"What do you want?"

"Pancakes?"

"Okay," she called.

Michael got cleaned up and collected clothes from the hamper to throw into the washing machine. He made a point of finding and including the UNC T-shirt with the load. He held the shirt for a second over the filling drum of the washer, then dropped it in.

"What's wrong?" Gail asked at the table, pancake on her fork.

Michael unscrewed the cap on the tin of syrup. "Nothing's wrong."

"Something's wrong. Is it the painting you're working on?"

"Nah." Michael took a bite. "These aren't bad." He paused. "Actually, work is going along pretty well."

"Good."

"I saw that guy's lawn mower this morning."

"Excuse me?"

"That beat-up mower he used on our yard. I saw it when I was running. I didn't see him, just the mower."

"Oh," Gail said. "And?"

"I saw it. That's it."

"Was it everything you expected?"

"Very funny," Michael said.

They were silent for a bit, then Michael said, "People used to believe that forces and spirits could enter into sculptures."

"I believe that. I believe that about your paintings," Gail said.

"They thought that the spirit the thing represented would enter it." Michael rubbed his temples. "I think I try to find spirits when I work. I think I'm looking for them."

"There's a lot of power in your work."

"I'm not talking about power." He didn't exactly snap, but he regretted the way he'd said his last words.

"I'm going to be late for class." She stood and grabbed her satchel from the counter, kissed Michael on the forehead.

"See you later," Michael said.

"I love you," Gail said.

"I love you, too."

Michael cleaned the kitchen and then went out to his studio. He turned on the standing fan and stood in front of it for a few seconds. He didn't work on the painting he had going, but took it from his easel and replaced it with a blank six-by-eight-foot canvas. He began to cry as he put blues on his palette: cerulean, cobalt—hue and color, pthalo, and indigo. He stared at the blank canvas, but was able to apply only one shade, cerulean. He started at the lower lefthand corner and moved slowly, with short strokes from a small brush, diagonally toward the upper righthand corner.

He went into the house to cool off and have a yogurt for lunch. He put the load of clothes into the dryer.

Back in his studio, Michael slowly pushed the cerulean into the canvas, scratching it in since there was so little paint on his brush. He'd always prided himself on the fact that, although he painted abstracts, he never began a canvas without a vision. That vision was subject to change, sometimes great change, but he usually knew what he wanted, what he was trying to express. This time was different. He pushed in more blue. Hours passed and the whole field was covered at last, blue and flat. He wanted to get far away from the canvas, far, far away, and try to see it like a piece of fallen sky. He recalled a Chinese thinker named Chhiao who claimed that from a certain distance a mirror could see a person, but that person would be unable to see the mirror. So, in fact, one could be someplace and not know it.

Back in the house, he decided on another run before Gail returned home from school. He grabbed the blue T-shirt and sprinted down the street toward the avenue, slowing as he neared the traffic. He crossed over to the next street and turned toward the hardware store where he had seen the silent man's mower. The mower wasn't there and Michael had to admit to himself that he was disappointed, although he was at a loss to say why. He continued his run, cutting it short and arriving home to find Gail's car in the driveway and the mower man at work on Michael's close-cropped yard.

"Did you tell him he could mow again?" Gail asked Michael as he came through the kitchen door.

Michael went to the sink for a glass of water, looked at her as he drank it all.

"Did you?"

Michael walked into the laundry room pulling off his shirt. He opened the lid of the washer.

"Michael?"

He dropped the shirt into the machine. "No, I didn't tell him he could do it."

"This is too weird. I'm calling the police."

"Let's ask him not to come back first," Michael said. "We haven't actually tried that yet."

"He's crazy." Gail leaned against the doorjamb. "He scares me, Michael."

"Okay, I'll talk to him."

Michael walked outside without a shirt and approached the man from behind as he was pushing and pulling the mower around a shrub. Michael tapped the wool-covered shoulder. The man turned without a start. Michael pointed to the machine, motioning for him to turn it off. The sound spiraled into silence as the two men just looked at each other.

"You're going to have to leave," Michael said.

The man stared at him.

"You do fine work, but you're going to have to leave. I'm not going to pay you for this."

He turned and reached for the pull start of the lawn mower.

Michael stopped him, grabbing the long-sleeved woolen arm. "No. You're scaring my wife."

The man looked at the house.

"You have to leave."

The man looked at his mower, at the house, and then at Michael.

"Please," said Michael.

The man dragged the machine to the sidewalk and walked toward the avenue, not looking back.

Michael went back into the house and said to Gail, "I think he got the message."

"Did you have to threaten him?"

"No."

"What did you say to him?"

"I simply told him that he wasn't going to be paid for the work and that we didn't want him coming back." Michael looked out the door window.

"My hero."

"Right."

Michael looked at the lawn, which had been cut day after day, and saw that nothing made it look any different. But something was better about it. He tried to see where the man had left off in the middle of the job, but there was nothing there, just grass the same height and green-turning-to-brown color everywhere.

Michael's run was slow. His knee ached slightly, but he pushed on, taking a different route. He came finally to the alley and there was the mower. It was later in the morning and the hardware store was open; rakes and spades and brooms had been pushed out onto the sidewalk as if they were things people bought on impulse. Michael walked inside.

"Do you know who owns that lawn mower in the alley?" he asked at the checkout counter.

"Lawn mower?" the man asked.

"It's parked right beside your store."

A teenager who was making keys said, "He's talking about Teddy's machine."

"Oh. That's Teddy's machine," the man said. "He works yards around here. Want to buy it?" He laughed.

"Where is Teddy?" Michael asked.

"He's around if his machine is out there."

"What do you know about him?"

The man gave Michael a long look. "There's not much to know. He mows people's yards."

"Can he talk?"

The man frowned. "I never heard him talk." He turned to the kid. "You ever heard Teddy talk?"

"Nope."

"Then how do you know his name?"

The man considered the question. "I don't know."

That night Michael held Gail's head against his shoulder in bed. He stroked her hair. "I love you," he said.

"I love you."

"No, I really love you."

"Well, I really love you," Gail offered, pretending to fight.

Michael fell into an awkward silence.

"What's wrong?" Gail asked.

"Nothing's wrong."

"Something's wrong."

"I just love you. Is that all right?"

Gail didn't say anything.

Michael lay awake for a while, feeling his wife's breathing, counting her breaths, her heartbeats.

Michael sat in front of the blue canvas. He didn't work. He just looked at the blue and waited for the sound of the mower out in his yard. He reached forward, touched the still wet oil color, and rubbed the pigment into his fingers. He often had the urge common to painters to eat the paint, and the urge had never been greater than it was now. He took a brush and put more cerulean onto the canvas. The added paint didn't change the blue on the canvas, didn't make it darker or more blue, but he continued to apply it: the same color over the same color. He licked the paint from the fingers of his left hand, felt the oil slide down his throat, and imagined it coloring the walls of his esophagus and stomach. With the blue that would not mark the blue on which he painted, he wrote that he loved his wife.

Michael had a vague, smudged recollection of Gail's face upside down, framed by her swinging hair. Her mouth was saying, "I love you, Michael." He left the memory and his eyes opened only to be bothered by bright sunlight. He knew from the quality of the light that his window faced west. The first thing on which he focused was the yellow plastic bracelet on his left wrist that read, LAWSON, MICHAEL, and he felt relieved to find that he was still himself. He looked toward the light and saw that the window was covered with a panel of wire mesh. Michael knew where he was and the rawness of his throat reminded him of what he had done. He was slightly surprised to find that he was free of constraints and that he was dressed in pajamas rather than a gown. There was a plastic pitcher and two plastic cups, one yellow and one red, stacked on the bedside table. Michael sat up and filled the yellow cup with water, although it was still stuck inside the red. He swung his legs around and let his feet touch the floor; his limbs felt unmanageable, heavy. His fingernails had been trimmed brutally short and the tips of his fingers ached. There was a square window in the door of the room with wire mesh in the glass, about nine-by-nine inches. No one was looking in from the other side: an absence Michael noticed with both fascination and despair. He looked at the portable toilet by his bed. He pushed himself to his feet and found his equilibrium, then negotiated the several steps to the door. He tried the knob to find it locked, then went back to his bed where he waited quietly, sitting with his knees pulled to his chest.

The tumblers of the lock fell, the knob turned, the door opened, and in walked a tall orderly, dressed in baby blue with a crease in his trousers. One hand held a tray and the other pointed a finger. "I knew you was up. How you feeling, brother man?"

"All right," Michael said.

"All right, then." The orderly put the tray down on the rolling table at the foot of the bed. "How's that throat?"

"Scratchy."

"Well, we got you some yogurt and some tapioca for dessert." The young man laughed, a snorting laugh. "Kind of a color-theme-thing going on, wouldn't you say?"

"I like yogurt," Michael said.

"Good." He looked at Michael for a long second. "Well, anything you want, you just ask Randy."

"Randy."

"Yeah, you just ask me. I got the joint wired."

"Can you get me a mirror?" Michael asked.

"Why you want a mirror?"

"I want to look at my throat. I want to see if it's blue."

Randy sighed and his manner changed. "Sorry, can't get you that. Your throat ain't blue, man."

"Thanks."

Michael watched the door close and listened to it lock, surprised by how little he felt, surprised by how uncrazy he seemed. He lay down on his side, put his head on the pillow, and faced the window, feeling the light through his shut eyes. He fell into sleep and started to dream. He was sitting under an oleander with a black dog that was not his, watching a parade of purple and house finches, jays, and finally, one rufous-sided towhee. He looked at the black dog and the animal looked at him. He stroked the dog's head while he turned his gaze up through the branches and leaves of the oleander. He found the blue of the sky.

When Michael awoke he was staring at an expanse of blue, but there was no wire mesh protecting it, no window holding it away from him. He sat up in bed and realized he was staring at his canvas set on an easel. There were two people in the room with him, a woman and a man, on each side of the painting.

"I'm Dr. Unseld," the woman said. Her hair was tied back and she wore a brown skirt and a tight white sweater.

"And I'm Dr. Overton," said the man, his bald head catching light from the ceiling fixture. His tie was loosened and his collar button undone.

Michael nodded, sitting up, rubbing his eyes, and making the sheet neat about his middle. "How is my wife?"

"She's fine," Dr. Overton said. "A bit concerned."

"I can imagine," Michael said.

Dr. Unseld smiled. "Do you remember this painting?" she asked, but didn't pause for an answer. "This is what you did before you ate the oil color."

Michael nodded.

"Do you recall eating the paint?" Dr. Overton asked.

"I think so."

"How do you feel about it now?" Overton asked.

"I feel fine. I'm sorry, I'm not really sure why I did it. Somehow work got the better of me." Michael looked at the canvas.

"Is that how you think of your work?" Unseld said, stepping away from the easel and closer to the bed. "As an adversary? As an enemy?"

"Sometimes."

"What were you thinking while you were eating the paint?" Overton asked.

"I don't know," Michael said, looking at the man's eyes. "This seems a lot like an ambush. I mean, to just wake up and find you in here with that thing."

"An ambush," Overton said. "So we're the enemy?"

"I didn't say that," Michael said, frowning a bit. "Listen, I did something that I shouldn't have done, something that doesn't make a lot of sense, doesn't make any sense. I realize that. But I love my wife. I like my life most of the time. I don't like being in here."

"Do you remember the man who mowed your lawn?" Overton asked.

"Yes."

"What do you remember exactly?" Unseld asked, sitting in the only chair in the room.

"What do you want to know? I can tell you what he looked like. Gail and I didn't really want him coming back like he did. Why are you asking me about him?"

"Just asking."

"Listen, am I allowed to go home?" Michael asked with a long sigh.

Dr. Unseld crossed her legs and leaned forward, resting her elbow on her knee and pinching the bridge of her nose. "That really depends on you," she said.

"You mean there's some sanity question that I can answer and then you'll unlock the gates?"

"You can see our situation, can't you?" This from Overton who was studying the canvas with his arms folded across his chest. "How do we know you're not still dangerous to yourself?"

"I guess you don't," Michael said. "But I'm not dangerous to anyone else. To tell the truth, it's none of your business if I want to kill myself. I may as well tell you that I wasn't trying to do that when I was eating the paint."

"What were you trying to do?" Unseld asked.

"I was trying to eat the paint," Michael said. "Stupid, I know, but I wanted to taste it. I looked at it and I wanted to eat it. Like I said, stupid."

Unseld and Overton looked at each other and seemed to communicate with their eyes. Unseld stood up from the chair and went over to Michael's side. "Don't worry," she said.

"What is your relationship with the color blue?" Overton asked.

"It's a primary color," Michael said. "Of course, that canvas is cerulean."

"Does that make a difference?" one of the doctors asked.

"In so far as it's not indigo or pthalo blue, I guess."

"I see," Overton said. "It's a kind of sky blue, isn't it? Does it make you think of freedom?"

"Not really. Do you think you might be overworking the loose associative stuff?"

Unseld smiled.

"So, can I go home?"

"We'll see." Overton said.

Michael nodded, deciding that to show anything less than calm forbearance and muted patience would certainly work against him. He was already sorry that he had slipped and referred to his work that way. But he also did not want them believing that he was acting out the role of the "compliant, good patient" in an attempt to deceive them. He found, however, as he laid his head back down, that he didn't care. His head was hurting rather severely, but it was a headache he recognized, had cataloged, and knew well, so it comforted him to have it. He took comfort in the very knowledge that so greatly concerned him previously, that as diagnosticians these people were Neanderthal.

Michael was awake and sitting up in the chair when the door was unlocked later that day for Gail. He stood and they embraced, lovingly, with mutual concern, but with a distance, not so much a coldness as an absence of heat.

"I'm sorry," Michael said. "I'm so sorry." He was hugging her tightly, speaking into her hair.

Gail pulled away from him and sat on the chair. "Are you okay?"

Michael walked to the window and looked out at the lights in the parking lot. "Yes, I'm okay."

"I'm scared," she said.

"I know. I wish I could take it away."

"I guess time will do that," she said, bravely, lying, not looking at him but at the bed. "You know, I really hate your head. I hate knowing it gives you pain and then I hate you sometimes."

"It surprises you that I understand what you just said?"

"You understand everything," she said. "You're too damn understanding."

Michael tried to be silent without giving the impression that he was withdrawing. He noted how his imprisonment was allowing him a certain perceptive distance, a mechanical or clinical eye that he found uncontaminated by his own wants and insecurities. Still, he was troubled by his indifference.

"I do love you," he said.

"Everything seemed to be going so well," Gail said, rubbing one eye.

"It was."

"Then what happened?" She looked directly at him for the first time and he found that a relief. "Tell me what happened, Michael?"

Michael sat on the bed, leaned forward, his hands clasped in his lap. "I don't know."

"Will it happen again?"

"No."

"How do you know?"

"I know," he said.

"You can't know. You didn't know this was coming, did you? Did you?" The anger was finding its way into her voice. She stroked her hair and pulled it behind her ear. "Will you talk to the doctors?"

"I've already talked to them."

Gail stood and Michael stayed seated. "They say you're coming home."

Michael nodded. "I want to come home."

"You conned them just like you conned me. Just like you con me every day. They like you, Michael. They think you're smart and funny and . . ." She stopped and bit her lower lip. "I'll see you tomorrow."

Turned Out

Lawrence Miller didn't balk at the draw. Balking wasn't going to do much good. He heard the muffled comments and the sighs, but he ignored them. Kemp Hollis pushed his chin away from his body and spat tobacco juice into the dust.

"That's a filthy habit," Lawrence said and leaned back against the booth of the concession stand.

"Ain't a habit."

Lawrence looked at him.

"A habit is something you have to do," Kemp said. "Chewing tobacco is something I want and choose to do."

"All day long, every day?"

"Damn near."

Lawrence thought again about the bull. "It'll be a short son-of-a-bitchin' ride at least." He smiled briefly. "Strike you funny that I'm the only black man here and I draw the monster?"

Kemp shrugged. "Somebody had to pull him."

Lawrence put a cigarette between his lips and stuck the pack of Old Golds back into his shirt pocket. He struck a match and held it in his cupped hand the way his uncle, who had been in the navy, taught him. "Ground's hard as hell today."

"Dry." Kemp looked at Lawrence. "That ever get you down? I mean, being the only black person somewhere? I never been the only white person, except when I was alone." Kemp laughed.

Lawrence shook his head, smiling.

Both nodded hello to a couple of passing men.

Kemp leaned out beyond the wall, watched the men walk out of earshot, and shook his head. "It's not going to be the same without Phillips and his kid in the team roping. They didn't ever win, but they was fun to watch."

"That's true enough."

"Phillips took it hard."

"Yeah, that was pretty tough."

"Fool kid," Kemp said and kicked the heel of his boot against the wall. He did it again. And again.

Lawrence watched the paint chips settle to the parched ground with each strike of the man's foot. "You keep that up and she's going to come out here and kick your ass."

Kemp continued to bang the wall.

There was a blur at the back of the booth. Most of the water hit Lawrence, cold against his neck and down his shirt. He hopped away. Kemp laughed and moved off as well. Lawrence looked to find Connie Flitner standing there with a large empty paper cup turned mouth down in her hand.

"Jesus, Connie," Lawrence said, pulling his shirt away from his chest. "That was cold."

"Quit kicking the wall," she said.

"Wasn't me."

"Quit kicking the wall." She pointed at both of them, her eyes in a squint.

"Have a little pity for the man," Kemp said. "He just drew the meanest, most ornery, ugly, and smelly bull in Wyoming. This man is going to ride Rank."

Connie tossed a new look Lawrence's way, licked, then bit her bottom lip, and crushed the paper cup in her hand. "You be careful, Lawrence Miller." She turned and started away, stopped and looked back. "You hear me?" She went back into the concession stand.

"She's sweet on you," Kemp said, resuming his position against the wall.

"Did you see the way she looked at me?" Lawrence looked at the sky. "Like I'm already dead. And it's a kinda pretty day. Ain't right."

"Make you nervous?"

"What?"

"You know, Connie, kinda liking you."

Lawrence shook his head. "Should it?"

"I was just wondering."

"Yeah, well."

Kemp looked at the distant hills. "Relax. You've ridden bad bulls before. Don't act like no baby in diapers, now. Killers, boy, killers. You've ridden killers. What about Prince? Remember him?"

Lawrence nodded.

"Rank ain't no worse than Prince."

Lawrence just looked at him. "Yeah, right. How come everybody's looking at me like I'm as good as dead?"

"You're just ugly," Kemp said.

"True."

They stepped around to the front of the concession stand and bought a couple of Dr. Peppers. Libby Flitner took their orders while her older sister put together burgers and hot dogs. The men then went to the fence and watched the calf roping. Willard Harvey had a calf lie down on him and he couldn't get the animal back to its feet so he could drop it again and tie it. "Pretend it's Lois," Kemp shouted and a couple of cowboys down the fence laughed.

Lawrence looked down and heard the thud of the calf hitting the ground when Willard finally succeeded. The ground didn't even want to give up dust, he thought, it was that hard, tight. It was supposed to be softer, should have been softer. His head hurt and the sun was beginning to bother his eyes, so he told Kemp he was going to find a place to take a nap.

Out in the parking lot, Lawrence smiled at a couple of girls too young to give him anything but trouble. He found his way to his pickup and stretched out in the bed. He closed his eyes against the bright sky, and pulled his hat down over his face, ignoring the grooves of the metal pressing into his back. He didn't want to ride that bull. He was scared, really scared. He didn't feel right and everybody knew it. He didn't have a good reason to get on an animal like that. Hell, you didn't ride in two-bit deals like that one for money. Maybe for some kind of stupid fun. Maybe for the attention of a woman, another stupid reason. He felt a bee land on his hand and he just lay still, hoping he wouldn't get stung. He fell asleep, thinking that if the bee failed to sting him it would be out of pity.

His sleep was a sound one, complete with a dream that he couldn't quite track down enough to enjoy or manipulate. He heard a voice coming from outside his head. It was the high-pitched whine of young Tim Giddy. Lawrence pushed his hat away from his face and felt the sunlight hit his lowered lids. He turned on his side and opened his eyes, finding the bed wall and a bit of rust he'd never seen.

"Wake up," Tim said again.

"Wake up," Lawrence muttered, trying to move away from the voice.

Tim reached a hand over and gave Lawrence's shoulder a shake. "They're about to start the bull riding. Kemp told me to come get you."

"Okay."

Tim Giddy left.

Lawrence sat up, then pulled himself out. He stretched and

looked down at his boots, checking to see if he was steady. He gave himself a quick sobriety test, putting his feet toe-to-heel, closing his eyes, and tilting back his head. He was fine. He stretched again and cracked his knuckles.

He reached back into his truck, collected his gloves, and shoved them into his back pocket. He strolled past the bleachers and into a crowd of cowboys at the deck. Dust floated in the air. He was up third. He watched the first rider get thrown in short order. The man ran clear without a problem. The clowns just stood where they were and the bull ran across the ring and out. He didn't see the second rider, but he heard the whooping and hollering and knew that the rider had stayed on for the full eight.

"Ready to boogie?" some wise guy asked, but Lawrence didn't see who it was and didn't care.

Lawrence held his eyes fixed on the bull's head. The bull was so still, dead still. The animal's side rose and fell slightly with steady, shallow breathing. Lawrence let himself down on the bull's back. He heard Kemp's voice somewhere far off asking him if he was all right, but he didn't answer. He considered it a damn fool question. The big bull didn't move even a tiny bit when Lawrence's butt settled on him. The men working the chute became nervous and silent. Lawrence could feel the muscles of the animal between his legs and under the knuckles of his open hand working under the rope. The frozen stance of the bull prompted one cowboy to lean low and catch a glimpse at the bull's eyes. The man came up shrugging.

Lawrence pounded his fist closed about the rope, stirring the smell of the animal so that it found his nose. He stared blankly at the back of the red bull's head. Somebody asked if he was ready and he gave a quick nod. He was ready, ready for the explosion, ready for the twisting, ready for the push of pain through his back, ready for the violent snapping of his neck. The bull was so still those seconds before the opening of the chute that he believed the animal could feel the rapid pounding of Lawrence's heart.

The gate swung open. The bull took a couple of easy steps and stopped, became dead in space. The onlookers in the stands made no noise. Lawrence was aware of their silence and even managed to look up at them. He chuckled inside his head; at least he had their attention. It amused him that he had time to think this, that he had time to think anything. He had expected the first twist of the bull to shake him silly; he'd even anticipated that the first twist would be to the right. When nothing came he felt lost, like when a train stops at night. The clowns walked softly around, their loose and colorful garments flapping with the steady breeze. One clown stopped and flailed his arms a couple of times, then appeared to become unnerved by the animal's face. Lawrence kicked the bull in the sides. Nothing. He felt empty, hollow. There he was a black man, still, forever and always, as good as naked in front of everybody. The sun was beating down on him, making him sweat. He could smell the bull again. It had been a lot longer than eight seconds and his hand was stiffening, but he was afraid to loosen his grip. It was a trick. He would loosen his fist and the beast would end his life, shake him off and gore him beyond recognition. He kicked again. Harder. He found the muscles of the bull tense, frightening. Everyone looking on was scared as well. He could sense it, taste it.

"Kemp!" Lawrence yelled, his eyes still on the bull's neck. "Kemp!"

"Yeah?" Kemp answered.

"What now?!"

There was no answer.

Ten minutes passed. Lawrence had time to pick out faces in the crowd, to nod to the familiar ones, but they were too terrified to notice. Connie was at the fence now, holding onto her sister.

He thought once that he felt the bull move, but there had been nothing, no dust rising from any hoof, no lingering ripple of a twitched muscle.

Lawrence took a long slow breath and as he let it out he loosened his grip slightly and the bull took a lateral step. The crowd sucked in wind collectively. Lawrence heard it and his fingers tightened again. A clown ran toward the bull and veered away quickly. The clown stopped and stood by a barrel, his chest heaving. Lawrence listened to the man panting. He swallowed. Another couple of minutes passed. Patient crowd, he thought. He also felt that he had had just about enough. In one quick effort he released the rope and pushed himself up and off the bull, rolling onto the hard ground and bolting away a few strides. He was still in the ring and the animal was still motionless, just looking forward. He walked around the animal, studied its back, and noticed just how big it really was, the muscles of the shoulders, the rump. He looked at the clown's face and saw his fear. He moved wide and came to stand by the barrel with the man. The bull's face was scary to see, blank, his eyes glazed over, unlike the dumb expression of a cow.

Lawrence turned to observe the people in the bleachers. They were still silent, standing mostly, and many had moved down to the fence. Lawrence stepped away from the barrel and stood in front of the bull. He was directly in front, not five feet away and the bull just stayed there, staring straight through him. He waved his arms, then he yelled. He yelled the bull's name. He yelled for it to do something. Finally, he turned his back on the animal and walked slowly, leisurely away toward the fence. His senses fused. He was ready for the snorting, for the sound of a stamping hoof or the beating of all the hooves against the stiff ground. Nothing. He reached the fence and climbed over. Sitting there, he looked back at the bull.

A cowboy swung open the gate at the far end of the ring and the bull trotted through it. People began to quietly leave the stands. The concession booth was already closed. Cars and trucks lined up to make the turn out onto the highway. The team-roping event had not come up and wouldn't. The hands were calmly clearing out the stock and moving it to the pens in back. Even the animals had become hushed, even sedate, their movements measured, methodical, deliberate.

Kemp came and slapped an arm over Lawrence's shoulder. "You okay?"

Lawrence nodded, then turned to look back at the empty ring. The dust had settled.

The Infirmary was at the edge of town, rustic and old-looking in spite of its newness. Lawrence nursed his second beer, sitting across a booth table from Kemp and Hank Fussey. Fussey was a large man, taking up more than half of the seat, pushing Kemp up against the wall. Lawrence thought to offer Kemp a seat on his side so that he might have some breathing room, but he knew the man would decline. Kemp wanted to see Lawrence Miller's face, to see the man's eyes.

"I ain't never been so scared in all my life," Fussey said, shaking his big head. "I thought you were a dead man. Sure as I'm sitting here."

"It was truly something," Kemp said.

Lawrence shook his head and drank from his mug of beer. He saw Connie Flitner come through the door. He smiled and nodded to her. She came over and said hello. Lawrence got up and asked her if she wanted to sit with them. She slid across the green vinyl seat. Lawrence looked to find Kemp smiling and offering a covert nod.

Lawrence caught a passing barmaid and ordered a beer for

Connie. He sat down and cleared his throat. "Lots of excitement today," he said.

"He's a brave man," Kemp said.

"Kemp, the bull didn't do shit." Lawrence glanced over at Connie. "Excuse me."

"I've heard the word shit before, Lawrence Miller. Been known to use it on occasion."

Lawrence studied his beer, tracing his finger about the rim of the mug. He stopped when he saw Fussey mimicking his action.

"Truly something," Fussey said.

The barmaid brought Connie's beer and left. Connie thanked Lawrence and took a sip. Her right hand was on the seat and had moved across the vinyl to Lawrence's hand. The backs of their fingers touched gently. Lawrence didn't take her hand, but he didn't move his away. He smiled at her.

Dean Phillips walked by and leaned over the table. "How are you gentlemen?" he asked.

"Doin' good," Kemp said.

Phillips slapped a hand on Lawrence's shoulder and looked at him. "How about you?"

Lawrence nodded.

Phillips gave his shoulder a squeeze and walked away to the table in the back where some of the older guys sat.

The booth was quiet for a while. Lawrence guessed that Connie, Fussey, and Kemp were thinking about Phillips's son. Lawrence was wondering why the man had a sudden interest in his well-being.

"Everybody's saying it's the damnedest thing they ever saw," Fussey said, his eyes locked on Lawrence. His pupils were covered with the shine of a few beers.

"Are you going to eat me or something?" Lawrence asked Fussey. "I mean, stop looking at me like that."

"What was it like?" Fussey asked.

"I'd rather not talk about it."

"Come on, Lawrence," Fussey pleaded.

"How did it feel?" Kemp asked, his voice low, his face leaning over the table.

Lawrence looked at the two men across from him and then at Connie at his side. She too was eager for some kind of answer. He drained his mug and set it down with a heavy fist for effect and leaned back into the seat. He looked at the people near the door and at the bar. Some were staring at him. All were aware of him. As always. "I felt . . ." He stopped.

"Yeah," said Fussey.

"I felt horny."

Kemp coughed out a laugh.

"Get outta here," Fussey said.

"No, really," Lawrence said. He was holding Connie's hand now.

Fussey was open-mouthed and wide-eyed. "You felt horny. You mean like . . ."

"Why do you think it took me so long to jump off, Hank?"

Fussey was shaking his head. Kemp was beginning to believe the story.

Lawrence was looking right at Fussey's eyes. "Really," he said.

Lawrence left the Infirmary alone after telling Connie he needed to drive and think. He was surprised at how stiff his body felt; the muscles of his thighs still felt cramped from having squeezed the bull so tight for so long. He fell in behind the wheel of his pickup and drove out of the dirt parking lot and back toward the arena. Connie had really wanted to be with him, but he wasn't ready.

He brought his truck to a stop at the stock pens and got out. The bulls lowed a bit, the broncs nayed and whinnied, and the calves bawled. The sounds were quiet sounds that belonged there. Music. He walked between pens and the horses stamped the ground nervously. The he saw the red bull, almost glowing under the moonlight. No, the animal did not have dull bovine eyes, but eyes almost like a cat's. He leaned on the fence and studied the bull.

"What is it with you?" Lawrence asked.

The bull stared at him, unmoving.

"I could have ridden you."

The bull took a step backward.

"Did you see their faces?" Lawrence laughed softly, shaking his head. "They were more scared than I was." Lawrence looked west at the field behind the pens and the stand of cottonwoods at the edge, the hills cut against the sky beyond it all. He walked the perimeter of the pen to the gate at back that opened to the west and the expanse of pasture. He swung out the gate. "Well, go on, crazy. Beat it. Hightail it! Hiya, get outta here!" Lawrence came around the gate and into the open.

The bull stepped back.

"The gate's open. Go." Lawrence stood in front of the bull, thinking he wished he were drunk just to have a decent excuse for standing there like a fool. He walked along the inside of the pen and tried to urge him out. "Get! Hiyah!"

The bull charged. Lawrence dove to the ground and rolled out of the way, and the bull ran on past and out into the field where he slowed to a walk.

Wolf at the Door

The last pink wash of daylight through the den window was no longer enough. Hiram Finch pulled the beaded chain on the green-shaded lamp beside the table and continued writing. His pen had moved fluidly from a rather controlled script to a loose scrawl that was allowing him only a few words per line. He paused, sipped his tea, then filled his cup again from the fat blue pot that had been a gift from an Australian couple who had come through with a sick horse a couple of years ago. He got up, opened the wood-stove, and laid the page down on the red-and-orange-glowing coals. He watched it catch flame and then closed the door. He heard the quiet steps of his wife approaching from the stairs.

"You need another log in the stove," Carolyn said, sitting down in the overstuffed chair and blowing on a mug of coffee. The aperture of her lips was perfect for playing her flute, which for so many years had lain idle in a drawer somewhere in the house. "I think it's colder in here than it is outside."

Hiram put a couple of small alder logs into the stove and poked at them with the iron, loosening the bark to allow the flames to lick through to the wood.

"I think you should just let it go," Carolyn said.

Hiram nodded and sat back at the table by the window, picked up the pen and tapped it against his corduroy leg. "I suppose that would be the wise and prudent thing to do."

"I suppose."

"This table is getting wobbly," Hiram said, grabbing it by the edge and giving it a small shake.

"You're just going to get all riled up and then they're going to do what they're going to do anyway." She blew on her coffee. "Just follow the path of least resistance for once."

"Just leave me alone. Please."

"Sure thing." Carolyn sipped from her mug.

"Listen, I'm sorry. I didn't mean it like that."

"Okay."

Hiram sighed. "Christ, I just apologized."

"And I said 'okay.' Okay?" Carolyn stood and looked about the room as if trying to remember some undone task. "I'm going upstairs to read for a while."

"All right."

Hiram watched her leave the room. He tossed the pen onto the table and looked out at the lavender-approaching-violet sky. He'd seen a falcon knife through the night out this window earlier, right across the moon like a ghost, and he wanted to see one now. Carolyn was probably right, he should just let it go. He couldn't stop them. The lion was indeed dangerous; any animal like that which wasn't terrified of people was dangerous. It apparently was not the least bit shy like other big cats. It came down to kill a lamb or a couple of chickens every couple of weeks and had nearly scared to death a teenage boy who was tending a fence. Although it was unclear whether the animal was actually interested in him, because in the boy's words it walked by "just as casual as anything." So they were going to kill him or her; no one knew the sex of the cat. They only knew that it killed and was large and wasn't much impressed by human presence. Hiram's irate and raging letter to the county commission wasn't going to stop them from putting a bounty on the lion's head. The crazy veterinarian who lived on the hill might be fine for looking into bovine eyes and studying the stool samples of sheep and horses and dogs, but what did he know about lions?

Hiram heard Carolyn upstairs in the study and felt bad for talking to her the way he had. He got up and climbed the stairs, leaned against the doorjamb, and watched her scanning the books in the case.

"I'm sorry about the way I acted," he said.

"That's okay," she said without looking up from the books.

"You're right about letting it go, you know."

"Whatever."

Hiram watched as she took a book and sat down on the love seat. "I'm going to check the horses." If she did offer a response, Hiram didn't hear her. He went back downstairs and left the house. He crossed the yard to the stables, finding as he entered that the horses were somewhat agitated, stepping back and forth and complaining a little.

"What's wrong, girls?" he said, turning on the lights and looking through the center of the barn and out the back. "What's got you all jittery?" He took the flashlight from the wall by the door and walked across the dirt floor, shining his beam into the corners of the stalls, and petting the noses of his horses. "No food now, silly," he said to his too-fat Appaloosa. He walked out the other side of the barn and shined the light into the corral, sweeping the baked hard ground for any sign, although he knew this was a wasted effort given the condition of the earth and his ineptitude as a tracker.

.   .   .

Hiram recalled when he was seventeen and his father's flock had been attacked by what was thought to be a wolf. Two lambs and two ewes had been torn to pieces and were strewn about the pasture nearest the house. That was the amazing part, that the carnage had been so close. Hiram's father was upset with eight-year-old Carla because she had the sheepdog sleeping with her in the house.

"At least, he would have barked and I would have known something was going on," Hiram's father said. He stood at the fence just outside the back door and looked out across the pasture. "Damn wolf."

"Zöe could have been killed, too," Carla said.

Hiram's father didn't respond. Hiram had been walking about the pasture. The sheep ran from him every time he drew near, still anxious, still bleating crazily. He was on the other side of the fence.

"Dad, I don't think it was wolves," Hiram said.

"And why do you say that?"

"A wolf wouldn't have killed so many animals."

"Wolves, then."

"Wolves don't kill like that. They would kill only the lambs and eat them; they wouldn't leave most of them lying all over the place. I think it was dogs. I think somebody's dogs got loose and went wild."

"You know as well as I do that there's a wolf around. You saw him with your own eyes up on the mountain."

"I think it's dogs." Hiram looked down at Carla and then at the border collie who was scratching her ear with a hind foot. "And I think they would have killed ol' ugly right there if she had been out."

"Zöe's not ugly," Carla said and she knelt to hug the animal around the neck.

Hiram's father was not much taken with the theory. He just muttered something about getting his rifle.

The following day, a fine rain fell and most of the mountain seemed unusually quiet. Hiram sat astride his horse, Jack, a twelve-year-old gelding who behaved as if he were three. He held his father's Weatherby rifle across his lap while he watched his father, who had dismounted and was poking through a pile of animal scat with a stick.

"Looks like dog," Hiram said.

Hiram's father nodded and climbed back into his saddle. "I don't know. Got hair in it."

They rode on up the mountain and Hiram recalled all the stories the Indians told about the wolf and its power and he wanted to believe that the animals were a part of the place, wanted to believe that he was a part of the place. His father and mother always laughed at him when he talked about such things, called him "youthful." Hiram didn't know any Indians but he had read a lot about them, especially the Plains Indians, and although he knew that his sources might be questionable, he still wanted to believe them.

"Dad," Hiram said as they topped a ridge. "Can't we just scare the wolf away?"

Hiram's father laughed. "You mean like reason with him?"

"What about getting one of those tranquilizer guns and relocating him?"

Hiram's father shook his head. "Where would we get one of them guns? Besides, we can't afford it. Nah. Anyway, a wolf ain't nothing but a big, evil dog."

. . .

The caked blood was still flowing slowly from the cuts across the backs of the palomino's hind feet. Hiram let go of the leg and stood away, perspiration dripping from his face. The woman holding the horse's halter stroked his nose and settled him down, making soothing sounds, the kind of sounds one reserves for animals. The horse had gotten tangled in some barbed wire.

"I could just shoot myself," the woman said.

Hiram shrugged. "Accidents happen to animals, too."

"It's my fault though."

"The wounds aren't too bad," Hiram said, coughing into a fist. "The worst part is across his fetlocks. I'm going to give him a shot of antibiotics and leave an iodine solution with you. Just dab it on twice a day. Might sting him a little."

"He's such a big baby," the woman said.

"Yeah, I know. It's because he's a male." Hiram reached into his bag for the antibiotic and syringe. "You can't blame yourself," he said. "What good does that do?" He filled the syringe, stood, and quickly stuck the horse's flank, pressing the plunger in. He saw the woman flinch. "Better him than you." Hiram had known Marjorie Stoval since she and her husband moved down from Colorado Springs six years before. He was used to seeing mainly her during his calls. The last few times Mr. Stoval had been conspicuously absent; the toy sports car that never seemed to go anywhere was now gone. He looked past the horse at the rolling pasture and the steep foothills behind it, ochre and red in the heat of early summer.

"You've got a sweet place here," Hiram said.

Marjorie nodded, stroked the blond horse's neck, pulling his mane with each pass. She seemed lost in thought. She was an attractive, young-looking woman, but Hiram believed from previous conversations that she was about forty-five, although there was not much gray in the dark hair she wore pulled back.

"Well, I guess I'm done." Hiram closed his bag and picked it up, yawned, and as he did, realized that it was a tick of his that surfaced when he was nervous.

"Tired?" Marjorie asked.

"I guess." As they walked back toward Hiram's truck, he said, "Other than the scratches, Cletus looks pretty good."

"My husband left me," Marjorie Stoval said abruptly.

Hiram swallowed and looked beyond his truck at the two-story log house. "Yeah, well, I suppose these things happen."

"He moved in with a young woman over in Eagle Nest. They live in a trailer. Can you imagine that?"

Hiram shook his head. At the truck he put his bag in the bed, pushed forward against the cab wall, cleared his throat, and turned to the woman. "My wife and I are pretty decent company. Why don't we call you and arrange a dinner over at our place?"

Marjorie paused as if considering whether the offer was some kind of mercy dinner, then said, "That sounds nice," in a non-committal way as she smoothed the hair back from her face.

Carolyn was painting a metal chair set on spread-out newspapers on the front porch. Hiram stopped and looked at her. He reached forward and wet his finger with the blue paint streaked across her forehead.

"I'm glad this stuff is water-based," she said, setting the brush across the open can and standing up straight. She stretched her back and smiled at him.

Hiram smiled back, remembering a time when they would have kissed, a time when he would be gone most of the day and would miss her badly and she would miss him, too. They used to talk a few times during his work day, but not now. Now, he simply came home, Carolyn smiled at him, and he smiled back.

"Anything interesting today?" she asked as she stepped back to scrutinize her work. "I don't know if I really like this blue. What do you think?"

"Blue is blue." Hiram stepped past his wife and into the house, putting his bag on the table just inside the door and walked into the den where he fell into the overstuffed chair in front of the woodstove. He glanced at the coffee table where there was a stack of journals he had been meaning to read, needed to read.

Carolyn came in and sat on the sofa. She was sighing and still stretching her back.

"Is your back all right?" Hiram asked.

"It's just stiff from squatting."

"Would you like me to rub it for you?" he asked, but he didn't really want to do it. He would have liked a back rub, but the offer was not forthcoming from Carolyn. He leaned his head back, briefly studied the ceiling, then closed his eyes.

"Maybe later," she said, her voice sounding far away. "I found a lump on Zack's belly this afternoon." Her voice was closer now. Zack was a one-hundred-twenty-pound mutt Hiram had brought home from the shelter about five years ago. "It's kinda big."

"Where on his belly?"

"Just above his tallywhacker," Carolyn said.

Hiram chuckled at the term. "How big?"

"Golf ball."

"I noticed it a couple of weeks ago. It's an umbilical hernia. I decided to leave it alone. It was about the size of a gumball then."

"Well, it's bigger now."

"I'll fix him up tomorrow. It's going to be a slow day. Yep, I'll just cut the ol' boy open and fix him right up."

Carolyn left the room. Hiram listened as she started to get dinner together in the kitchen. He went to help, the way he helped every night. The accounting firm where Carolyn once worked had folded and she hadn't found a new job. It had been two years and she'd pretty much resigned herself to not finding anything, so she had stopped looking. Hiram didn't care. They had enough money. They didn't do much traveling. But he hated her periodic complaining about being a housewife. He would respond by saying that he didn't think of her as a housewife, but rather a full-time gardener/painter/wrangler/everything else. He'd point out how much money she was saving them by doing what someone else would charge a bundle to do. But she still complained while doing nothing about it. He walked to the kitchen cupboard for the dishes.

"I was over at the Stoval place today," Hiram said. "Did you know that Mr. Stoval just up and left?"

"Really?"

"Mrs. Stoval told me. I guess she doesn't have many people to talk to, being out there all by herself."

"She was lucky you were there, wasn't she?"

Hiram set the plates on the table and looked at Carolyn. "Anyway, I mentioned that we might have her over for dinner."

"How nice."

"What is it with you? If I were talking about Mitch Greeley or old Mrs. Jett, you wouldn't sound like this."

Without looking away from the pasta on the stove, Carolyn said, "I don't guess we'd be having the same conversation about them."

"We don't have to invite her."

Carolyn turned off the flame under the pasta, then drained off the water in the sink before turning to Hiram. "I'm sorry. I'm tightly wound today. I think I'm feeling cooped up or something."

"Want to go out? Drive to town and take in a movie?"

Carolyn shook her head.

"What about an early morning walk up to the falls?"

Carolyn smiled in weak agreement.

An hour after dinner someone rang the bell. Hiram and Carolyn were reading in the den. Hiram was just beginning to nod off; the journal was resting on his lap. Carolyn looked at him as if to say, who could that be? and didn't move. Hiram got up and went to the door, opened it, and found Lewis Fife, all three hundred pounds of him standing on the porch.

"Well, they did it," Lewis Fife said quickly. He was out of breath, panting.

"You didn't walk over here, did you?" Hiram asked.

"Are you crazy? Of course not. I drove, but I took your steps two at a time," Lewis Fife said.

"There's only four steps, Lewis."

"Give me a break, man. I weigh a ton. You try hauling this shit around." He grabbed his stomach and showed it to Hiram. "Are you going to let me in?"

Hiram stepped aside and called back to Carolyn as the big man entered. "It's Lewis."

Carolyn came and stood in the doorway to the den. "Good evening, Lewis," she said.

"Ma'am," Lewis said and tipped a hat he wasn't wearing. "Well, they've done it," he said again.

"Done what?" Hiram asked.

"They killed that cat. Trevis Wilcox and his boy shot him up in Moss Canyon and just now dragged him down. They're down in the village at the grocery-store parking lot. I thought you ought to see it."

"Why?"

"Christ, man, you're the vet around here. Not that you can help the beast now, but take a look at it and tell us if you think it's the right cat."

"The right cat? I never saw it."

Lewis Fife bit his lip and said slowly, "Well, the Newton kid said the cat he saw was a lot bigger and, you know, when you're scared everything looks bigger, but still."

"Okay, I'll come down." Hiram turned to Carolyn. "Do you want to come with me?"

"I don't need to see a dead lion. I don't think you need to see it either."

"Probably not, but I'm going anyway." Hiram looked at Carolyn's face. She disapproved, but he could see that she was not up to an argument.

"Please don't get all upset."

"I won't."

"I'll take care of him," Lewis Fife said.

.   .   .

Hiram and his father searched all day, went home, and then returned to the woods the following morning. Hiram watched his father's face as they rode, his chin and cheeks darkened by a thick stubble. He didn't much like his father, not because he was a bad man, not because he was mean, but because he never seemed to want more for himself, never opened books, and seemed afraid when Hiram did.

"So when we find him, Hiram, I'm going to let you have him," his father said.

"I don't want him, Dad." Hiram sucked in a deep breath. "You know, Dad, there's probably not ten wolves left in these parts. We shouldn't be killing them."

"You're gonna shoot him, all right. It'll be kind of a rite of passage for you."

Hiram didn't say anything, but a chill ran through him and he felt like crying.

From up high they could look down to the beaver pond. There were no animals around and Hiram got a bad feeling that the wolf was near. They rode down the slope slowly. Hiram's father carefully pulled his rifle from its scabbard.

And there it was. The wolf was trotting along the near side of the pond, moving upstream. His coat was dark gray and he was carrying his bushy tail high. It was a big wolf. Hiram guessed that the animal weighed over a hundred pounds. It was beautiful, moving effortlessly. He loved the wolf. And when he looked at the smile on his father's face he was filled with hate. He was embarrassed by the hatred, afraid of it, sickened by it, feeling lost because of it.

"Come on, boy," Hiram's father said.

Hiram followed reluctantly. They rode down across the meadow and past the pond and then circled wide away from the creek and back to it. The wolf was standing in a thicket, just thirty yards away. Hiram could see his eyes, the rounded tops of his ears.

"He's all yours, boy," Hiram's father said.

"I can't do it," Hiram said.

"Shoot him," the man commanded. "Shoot him or you ain't no son of mine."

Hiram looked at his father's unyielding eyes.

"Shoot him."

Hiram raised the Weatherby and lined up a shot. The wolf didn't move; his eyes were as unyielding as his father's. He squeezed off the round and watched as the startled animal had only enough time to change the expression in his eyes. The wolf looked at Hiram and asked why, then fell over dead as the bullet caught him in the chest with a dull thump. A shockingly small amount of red showed through the fur.

Hiram turned to his still-smiling father and said, "I hate you."

"Fine shooting."

"You didn't hear me," Hiram said. "I hate you." He stared at his father until the man looked away. Hiram turned his horse and stepped off in the direction of the pond.

"You had to do it, Hiram. That wolf was threatening our welfare, your family," the man called after. Then, more to himself, he said, "He was killing our stock. He had to be done away with."

Hiram rode home alone, feeling scared of what his father would do when he arrived, feeling scared by what the lost spirit of the wolf was going to do to him. Tears began to slide down his face and he wished that his father could see them.

As he rode down the steep ridge above his family's home Hiram saw them in the pasture. Six dogs were chasing a small ewe, sliding on the wet grass as she made her sharp turns. Hiram was filled with such anger that he couldn't breathe, his hands mindlessly raised the rifle, and he found himself drawing a bead on one dog and then another. He fired and missed badly, but the dogs went running away. He looked up the ridge and saw his father staring down at the dogs, staring down at him. Hiram gave his horse a kick and trotted home.

He didn't speak to his mother as he stormed into the house and he felt bad because he could tell he was frightening his younger sister, sitting there at the bottom of the stairs, stroking the border collie. He marched up to his room and slammed the door. He paced from the window to the door, his hands closing and opening, closing and opening, and all he could see was the face of the wolf, indifferent and unsuspecting, the amber eyes boring into him. He wanted to scream. He heard his father's horse outside and he looked through the window to see him tying up at the post.

"I hate you!" Hiram shouted, but his father didn't look up. "I told you it was dogs! I told you!" Still his father did not raise his eyes to the second floor, but walked onto the porch and into the house.

Hiram could hear his mother asking what had happened as he threw open his bedroom door and stepped to the top of the stairs. "*He's* what happened!" Hiram said. "He made me shoot that wolf."

"That's enough, Hiram," his father said.

"No, it's not enough. You made me kill that beautiful animal because you're too stupid to listen to anybody."

Hiram's father started toward him, up the stairs. It might have been the perspective, but Hiram realized that he was larger than his father. He looked down at the man and moved to meet him on the stairs.

"Hiram," his mother complained.

His sister was crying and that was the only sound which seemed to filter through his rage.

"I said 'enough,'" his father said.

"Bastard."

Hiram saw the rage in his father's eyes and ducked his swinging fist, heard his mother's scream. Hiram grabbed the man and felt how weak he was. He now understood that his father had been profoundly affected by the death of the animal, and felt his father's chest heaving with sobs. Hiram fell to the floor holding his father, both crying, neither letting go.

.   .   .

It was true that Lewis Fife didn't look comfortable seated in the driver's seat of an automobile. His stomach pressed against the steering wheel, which he held with both of his fat paws, the seat belt idle beside him since it would not accommodate his girth. "Been driving for thirty-five years and not one accident," Lewis Fife would say, taking a steep curve on two wheels. Hiram sat beside him in the monstrous mid-seventies Lincoln Town Car, squeezing his nails into the armrest, believing, as did everyone else, that Lewis Fife was long overdue for a vehicular mishap. But that night the fat man didn't take any curves on two wheels, didn't drive well above the limit, didn't crowd the center line, didn't fumble with a bag of chips set on his shelf of a stomach. Lewis drove steady and slow from Hiram's house all the way to the village with his eyes stapled to the highway; the silence about him suggested reverence. Hiram was taken over by a similar quiet mood. All he could imagine was the large, majestic, dead face of the lion.

Lewis Fife pulled into the parking lot of the grocery store and parked in a space well away from a large huddle of people. They were standing around the bed of a black dually pickup with yellow running lights.

Lewis Fife pointed but didn't say anything.

Hiram grabbed the handle, opened the door, and got out. He walked toward the truck, feeling the muscles in his stomach shaking as if he were freezing cold. Beyond the crowd and the truck was the market, all lit up; people inside were pushing carts and standing in the checkout lines. He looked at the people inside, trying to distract himself, trying to tell himself that there was other business in the world. He recalled the look on Carolyn's face as he left the house and repeated to himself that he wouldn't cause a scene.

Hiram heard someone say, "Hey, it's Doc Finch." And the crowd of men peeled away from the truck and watched him. He got to the bed of the big pickup and there it was. Nothing could have prepared him for the face of the animal. He was large, his head about the size of a big boxer dog's, and the front legs were crossed in a comfortable-looking position as he lay on his side. But the face. The mouth was open, showing pink against white teeth, and the tongue hung crazily out along the metal of the truck. The ochre eyes were open and hollow and cold and held a startled expression. Hiram looked up at the faces of the surrounding men, one at a time until he saw Wilcox and his son. The two were not quite smiling.

"We got him, Doc," Wilcox said.

Hiram swallowed. "Yep, I guess you did." Hiram touched the fur of the lion's neck and stroked it.

"Big one, ain't he, Doc?" someone said.

Hiram felt Lewis Fife standing beside him. He walked away from him, circled around the open tailgate of the truck, and studied the cat. "He's a big one, all right. I hope he's the right one."

"He's the right one," Wilcox said.

"Got him in Moss Canyon," the Wilcox son said. "I shot him," proudly, a little too loudly.

Hiram looked up, caught the boy's eyes, and saw the fear in them.

The silence was then broken by a scream and the breaking of glass. Hiram turned with the others to see Marjorie Stoval a few yards away, with dropped sacks and broken bottles at her feet, looking at the lion. She screamed again and then sank to her knees, crying. Hiram went to her, as did the Wilcox boy. Hiram supported her while the boy gathered her groceries. They helped her away from the pickup and to the line of stacked wire carts in front of the store.

Hiram talked to her. "Mrs. Stoval, are you all right? Mrs. Stoval?"

The Wilcox kid backed away and rejoined his father. Hiram stood with the woman and watched the crowd disperse, watched the black dually pickup drive off down the street.

"I'm sorry you had to see that," Hiram said.

Lewis Fife came over. "Is she okay?" he asked Hiram.

Hiram shrugged.

"I'm sorry," Marjorie said, trying to stand up straight, but keeping a hand on the cart. "I've never seen anything like that."

"I know. Where's your car?" Hiram asked. Marjorie pointed across the lot toward a small station wagon. "Listen, I'm going to drive you home."

"I'll follow you," Lewis Fife said.

The headlights of the Lincoln faded and grew large, but stayed in sight the whole way. Hiram had failed to adjust the driver's seat of Marjorie Stoval's wagon and so he was crammed in behind the wheel; his knee raked his elbow every time he shifted. Marjorie was no longer crying, but sat stone-faced, staring ahead through the windshield.

"Are you okay?" Hiram asked.

"I'm so embarrassed," the woman said.

"Why should you be embarrassed? I think your reaction was the only appropriate one out there. I told them not to, but they did it. They say they did it to protect their stock. They say they did it to protect their families. But none of that is true. They did it

because they're small men." Hiram felt how tightly he was holding the steering wheel in his hands, and when he glanced into the
mirror, he noticed that Lewis Fife's headlights were white dots
well off in the distance. He eased his foot off the accelerator and
tried to relax.

"You're really upset, aren't you?" Marjorie said.

Hiram didn't answer, but did look at her.

"That was a beautiful animal," she said.

"Yes, it was."

"I saw a lion near my place once." Marjorie rolled her window
part way down. "He was on the ridge about three hundred yards
from my house. I couldn't believe it. It was about nine in the
morning and I had just finished my tea and there he was. Or she. I
don't know. I got my boots on as fast as I could and went hiking
up there, but it was gone. I can still see the white tip of its tail." She
closed her eyes.

Hiram looked over at her face, the curve of her nose, then down
at her hands, large for a woman her size, but they fit her. "They're
magnificent creatures, all right. *Felis concolor*."

"I'm sorry you're having to do this, drive me home, I mean."

"It's no trouble." Hiram glanced behind them. "Besides, Lewis
is here to drive me home." He felt a cramp start in his leg and tried
to stretch it out.

"You're kind of wedged in there."

"Yes, ma'am."

Marjorie laughed.

"I like you, Dr. Finch," she said.

Hiram nodded and smiled at her.

"I'm sorry I unloaded my baggage on you earlier." Marjorie's
voice didn't sound frail anymore. "I mean, about what's-his-name."

"Eagle Nest, eh?"

"In a trailer." She shook her head. "Did I mention that she's twenty-three? I saw her. Dwight and I were shopping and we ran into her. She saw him and said hello and then she saw me and they pretended not to know each other. That's how I found out." She sneezed out a laugh.

"That sounds awful."

"Have you ever had an affair?"

"No."

"Ever thought about it?"

"No. I guess I'm pretty boring, huh?"

"I wouldn't say that," Marjorie said. "I wouldn't say that at all. In fact, I'd say you are anything but boring."

"Why, thank you kindly, ma'am."

Hiram turned off the road into Marjorie Stoval's yard and killed the engine. They were out of the car when Lewis Fife came to a complete stop. The fat man waited in his car while Hiram helped Marjorie with her groceries. He held the ruptured sacks and stood next to her on the porch while she looked for her keys. Once inside he put the groceries on the table in the kitchen.

"Well, I guess I'll see you around," Hiram said.

"I guess."

"Good night, Mrs. Stoval."

"Marjorie."

"Hiram." He smiled at her. "Good night."

Lewis Fife was more relaxed during the drive home than he had been during the ride to see the lion. He drove faster, his fat fingers holding the bottom of the steering wheel lightly.

"Seems like a nice woman," Lewis Fife said.

Hiram agreed.

"I never met her before tonight."

Hiram glanced out the window at the river as they passed it.

"I've been out to treat her animals a few times. I was out at her place treating her horse just today."

"She live there by herself?"

"Yes, I believe so."

"Not married?"

Hiram shrugged. He didn't want to seem removed, but neither did he want to broadcast the woman's life story all over the county. "I think there's a Mr. Stoval, but I've never seen him."

"Funny," Lewis Fife said, "the things we assume."

Hiram looked back out his window and his thoughts turned to the lion. "I wanted to scream just like she did," he said. "I just don't get people. Did you see the look on the Wilcox boy's face?" He glanced over at the silent Lewis Fife. "He hurt that boy."

"Takes all kinds."

At home, Hiram found Carolyn already in bed and sound asleep. He didn't pause for the cup of tea he wanted, just undressed and slid into bed next to her. He felt the cool sheets against his back and stared up at the ceiling. The vapor lamp over the door of the barn always threw just a little light through the window. He listened to his wife's breathing and closed his eyes. *The world was thirty inches high and full of scents, the pads of his paws struck the ground fully, completely, feeling it thoroughly, absolutely, pushing it away beneath his body with each stride and he was floating, the muscles of his haunches and shoulders replete with eager power, power resting, power tightly wound, his nerves on fire, his eyes pressed to the edge of capacity and all of it, all of it set to the quiet his presence created in the woods, the quiet and his subdued, continuous, vibrating breathing. He understood that he was in danger, that he fell centered in the crosshairs of someone's sad and human weapon, but he could not pause to be apprehensive, could not pause to locate the enemy, but instead walked through the woods that were his, the quiet of his making, looking for life where life always was, walking on the floor that had always been his, waiting for the report to split the air. Now he was Hiram Finch and he was standing in Marjorie Stoval's kitchen, at least he believed it was Marjorie Stoval's kitchen, it being oddly made of wood with the bark still on it, and Marjorie was standing in front of him, her blouse open and her breasts exposed and he was attending to her nipples, large nipples, the kind he had never found appealing, but here they were and he wondered why he was in her kitchen and she was pushing her finger toward him, toward his chest that he realized was uncovered, to his sternum. Her finger landed lightly and he could feel his heart rattling in its cave, vibrating and filling his torso with that low, continuous purring and her finger dragged its nail down along the line that separated his left from his right.* . . . Hiram awoke with a start and saw the light from the vapor lamp still on the ceiling and heard his wife breathing beside him. He pushed the top sheet off his body and tried to let the air through the window cool him. He was afraid and lonely and hungry, terribly hungry. He rolled onto his side and faced his wife's back. He put his hand on her hair.

Dicotyles Tajacu

Michael Lawson didn't believe his wife when she told him that she was tiring of his periodic depressions, nagging headaches really, bouts that would often last for a couple of weeks. The headaches manifested themselves in overly quiet behavior and some grumpiness, but mostly in minor absent-mindedness and seeming apathy. He didn't believe Gail when she said that she didn't like the way he talked to her when he was "lost in his own little world," nor when she informed him that she was falling out of love with him, although he had actually noted the germinating distance in spite of his ostensible lethargy and inattention. He didn't believe any of it when the message was conveyed by a "concerned" third party, his wife's friend Maggie, who had never seemed to like Michael anyway. Maggie made a special trip over for a chat, knowing that Gail was not there, and in fact admitted early on in the chat that Gail was waiting at her house. It didn't appear to bother Michael that Gail had a new close friend named Bob who was "fun" and "bright" and single, although the friendship hadn't, contrary to Maggie's accusation, gone without regard. He was some kind of skin doctor who lived way out with other skin doctors in a cul-de-sac in the foothills north and west of Denver. But when Michael came into the house from his studio, which was just seventy yards away, and found that all of the spots where the furniture had been were now merely spots, he could only do what the note on the bare wood of the kitchen floor said —"Believe it."

Michael didn't go to the foothills to talk to Gail, or to finally get a good look at Bob the skin doctor and his house with the bathroom the size of a barn. She left in the middle of one of his depressions and he somehow wanted her to be okay, at least he talked himself into believing that was what he wanted. He folded the note neatly and placed it on the counter. He thought perhaps he had never really loved Gail, and was saddened by the knowledge that she had loved him, had wasted her time loving him. Michael walked back out to his studio and collected his paintings, twenty-seven large canvases. He heaped them in a pile in the yard, doused them with gasoline from a can he kept for the mower, and tossed on a strike-anywhere kitchen match that he held until he burned his fingers. It was a big fire that caused a neighbor to call the fire department, who put it out quickly with fat hoses stretched across the yard, red lights twisting in the predawn sky, while the marshall wrote out a citation for Michael. When the fire fighters roared away, he packed all the clothes he could into the two suitcases that his wife had left behind, got into his pickup truck, looked into his mirror, and saw that a smattering of neighbors were still rooted, loitering and gawking and whispering. He then drove away, stopping at an automatic teller before heading north toward Wyoming.

For years, doctor after doctor had said, "We have to do something about your headaches," and let that pass as treatment. Finally, failed drug after failed drug, and one neurologist's insipid question, "Are you sure they're headaches?" led Michael to give up and admit that the pain was a part of his life. Evidently the headaches were not going to kill him, a lamentable thought, so he decided to get to know them, to feel them, to accept them, to, in what he thought was the Zen way, become one with them. He didn't mention them, just endured them. He didn't miss them when they left, and was not surprised when they returned: different headaches with disparate associative symptoms, which located themselves in various parts of his head, where they moved, pulsed, or sat immobile for hours behind an eye or ear like cheetah watching gazelle.

Michael drove north on Interstate 25, then west toward Fort Collins. Clouds were already collecting over the front range, just a few then, but soon there would be many, and he was glad to be out of Denver where the weather was always sudden and extreme: hail and tornadoes or clear, blizzards followed by sunny days of sixty degrees with gentle breezes from the south. He made his way through Fort Collins and stopped for breakfast at a diner on US 287 that sported stuffed animals everywhere he looked: heads of deer, elk, and moose were hung over the tables of booths, and bobcats, coyotes, and badgers marched along a mantle that separated the dining area from a little store with cold drinks, doughnuts, and sundries. The headache he nursed was a sharp, needling pain behind his left eye that spread toward the back of his head like smoke, becoming duller, but fingering out with a scratching at the base of his brain. He cataloged it as he fell into a booth beneath the head of a wild boar with a conspicuously missing left eye. The brass plate under the trophy read, "Javelina, *Dicotyles tajacu*, taken July 1967, Red River, NM by C.C. Wilcox."

The waitress, a plump woman, looking to be near thirty, was wearing off-white nurse's shoes and a too-short navy skirt and holding a pot of coffee. She said, "You can sit somewhere else, if you want."

Michael looked at her.

"If the *Dicotyles tajacu* bugs you," she said. "You can move to another booth. The *Odocoileus hemionus* is available. So is the *Antilocapra americana*."

Michael looked at the other dead animals over the empty booths. "I'm okay here," he said, turning his cup mouth up for the coffee.

"A lot of people don't like the *Dicotyles tajacu*," the woman said as she poured. "That missing eye."

"I see."

She pulled a menu from the large front pocket of her apron and set it on the place mat in front of him.

"You know all of these animals?"

"They're here everyday, all day long. I'm here everyday, all day long. You hunt?"

Michael shook his head.

"I'll come back for your order."

Michael studied the pig. At that moment, Gail was probably in bed with Bob having her skin examined. He recalled when he and Gail had first met: she had claimed to understand his pain, claimed she wanted to be near it, and wanted to watch him at work. They were standing in front of a canvas of Michael's at an exhibition of his in Santa Fe.

"There's so much pain in it," Gail said from behind him as he faced the painting.

Michael turned and looked at her. "Where?" he asked.

"Everywhere," she said.

"I don't see it," he said.

Gail was confused, but pressed on. "Here," pointing to a sweep of maples edged with Indian Yellow across a field of pthalo blue. "Here, this looks like acute pain to me, like intense loss."

Michael looked where she pointed, got up close, and touched the paint with his fingers. "You don't really believe that shit, do you?" But when he looked back at her face he saw she was near tears. "I'm sorry," he said. "You're right about the pain." A lie only because he believed that indeed he was lying every time he attempted to articulate how painting made him feel. In the middle of putting the paint on the canvas, when the desire to slide a razor across the arteries of his forearm was large and explicit before him, he recognized the urge as indulgent and decided it was made up, thought no one really had such feelings and so would sit down, leaving the work alone and rub his temples until he forgot his bad mood. But as Michael said to Gail that she was correct about the emotion she saw in his picture, he felt pleased to be able to share the pain. He was genuinely interested in this woman and what she was saying, but he also experienced considerable guilt because he knew that he was viewing this conversation as a hasty way to get her into bed.

"I'm Gail Lybrand."

"Michael Lawson."

"I know."

They had sex that night and continued to have sex for eight years and in that time Michael had sex only with Gail, although he was tempted once to be unfaithful with an anthropologist whom he'd met in the hills south of Santa Fe, but didn't because the thought of sex with another woman made his head hurt more and more and he took the pain as a sign. And so he went home to his wife of seven months and found that his headache didn't go away, but in fact got worse, and then Gail became angry with him because he was too sick to make love.

"What's this?" Michael said, looking at the chocolate-covered doughnut the waitress put on the table. The doughnut had been microwaved and the brown veneer had become thin on top and formed a series of puddles around the circle.

"On the house. Because you don't hunt." The waitress pulled her pad from her apron pocket and took the pen from behind her ear. "What'll it be?"

"How much for the pig?" Michael asked, surprising himself.

"Excuse me?"

"The head." Michael pointed up. "I think I'd like to buy it."

"The *Dicotyles tajacu*?"

"Yes."

"You want to buy the *Dicotyles tajacu*?"

"I believe that's what I'm saying."

The waitress tapped her pad with her pen and looked at the boar's head as if for the first time, then turned and walked away across the room and into the kitchen. The single door swung after her with a barely audible squeak. The bearded face of a large man suddenly appeared from the kitchen and disappeared just as quickly. Then all of him appeared, dressed in white or what was once white. Michael liked the stains on the man's clothes, ochre and Permanent Rose and a deep green like an avocado's skin.

"Waitress tells me you want to buy the *Dicotyles tajacu*," the cook said.

Michael nodded, but felt a little afraid sensing the man's displeasure.

"Why?"

"Because I like it," Michael said.

The cook sat across from him in the booth and looked absently across the room and out the window at the highway. "I've never had anybody wanting to buy one of the animals before. What would you do with it?"

"I'm an artist. I just like it. I wouldn't do anything to it," was what he said, but he wanted to say that he was unsatisfied, agitated, desolate in heart and entrails, sick with pain, and sickened by curiosity, of all things, and that the *Dicotyles tajacu* had become an object of that sickness. "I'm not going to hurt it."

"He's got an eye missing," the cook said. "The left one."

"I realize that," Michael said. "I think that's why I like it so much."

The cook scratched his thick neck and pulled up at the back of his shirt collar. "The *Dicotyles tajacu* has been here since 1967."

"Taken by C.C. Wilcox," Michael said.

"You know, business has been pretty rough, what with the freeway and all those fast-food places in Fort Collins. A breakfast bur-rito. An egg McNuthin'. It's hard for the little guy to make it now."

Michael nodded. "Are you C.C. Wilcox?"

The cook shook his head. "Kirk Johnston."

"My name is Michael Lawson."

The cook stared off into space.

"I can see you're attached to the pig . . ."

"*Dicotyles tajacu*," the cook corrected.

"*Dicotyles tajacu*," Michael said. "How does one-fifty sound?"

The cook looked up at the head on the wall and his eyes seemed to well with tears, the meaty fingers of his right hand were wring-ing the meaty fingers of his left. "Business has been awful slow." But the cook was speaking more to the taxidermied head than to Michael.

"One seventy-five," Michael said.

The man was openly weeping now. His big head fell forward to his hands; his big sides were heaving under his short-sleeved white shirt. The waitress had come out of the kitchen and was walking across the room, tossing them a sidelong glance but not approaching. A man with blond hair and his blond wife, who were seated across the room in a booth beneath a moose, stared and whispered.

Through his tears, Kirk the cook managed to say, "Would you consider the *Ovis canadensis*?"

"No, I want this one," Michael said. The idea of owning it was getting all twisted inside him. He didn't want to hurt the cook, but the head, the head, the idea of the head was calling to him. "Two hundred."

The cook let out a loud wail. His sobs caught in his throat, choking him; tears were glistening in his beard.

The blond couple from across the room climbed out of their

booth and scurried out. The bell hanging from the door was slapping against the glass.

"Two hundred dollars."

"Waitress," the cook called. When she came he said, still crying, "Wrap up the *Dicotyles tajacu*."

The waitress began to sob as well, her mascara streaking quickly as she turned her face from the stuffed head. Her crying voice was higher pitched than her talking voice and Michael paused to observe this.

The cook stood. "Wrap it nicely, waitress."

Michael counted out two hundred dollars onto the lacquered wooden tabletop. The cook picked up the bills along with a paper napkin and, without counting, stuffed the money into his breast pocket, then walked on unsteady legs back across the room and through the swinging door of the kitchen.

Michael moved his coffee to the next table. Then he and the waitress stood on the maroon vinyl seats of the booth, on each side of the boar's head, and took it down from the nail on which it was hooked.

"I'm going to miss you, *Dicotyles tajacu*," the waitress said. "I'll get some newspaper." She stepped back and looked at it there on the table before walking away.

Michael was able to examine the head more closely now. The hair was worn away on top of the skull between the eyes, and the tusk on the right side was broken. The surface of the protrusion was Indian Red and mustard. The hole where the left eye had been, and later whatever kind of glass ball had replaced it, was full of caked dust and cobwebs. He imagined the pain when the wind blew through an empty socket to the exposed nerves.

The waitress returned with a stack of *Rocky Mountain News* and spread a few sheets out on the floor. She made a mat using masking tape to secure the seams. Michael regarded how carefully she worked, as she kept adding more paper. Her hot-pink-painted nails sliced the tape precisely; the palms of her small but fleshy hands pressed the adhesive flat as the plane of paper grew into a rug. Michael stood, lifted the head from the table, and set it down. The two of them stepped back and studied the head.

The waitress got back down on her knees and brought the opposite edges of her newspaper rug up to meet at the bald spot between the eyes. She taped it closed, then proceeded to fold shut the gaps by using more paper until finally the *Dicotyles tajacu* was securely wrapped.

"I never did get anything to eat," Michael said, looking at the waitress. "I don't imagine it would be a good idea to order something now."

The waitress didn't say anything, nor did she move her head or any other part of her round little body, but she made it clear she was in agreement.

Michael picked up the head; the newspaper crackled in his arms. "Okay, then. Thanks." He left the restaurant struggling with the door; the bell hanging from the door handle hushed as it caught between his thigh and the glass. Michael put the pig on the passenger seat of his truck. He left it wrapped in spite of his urge to open its one-eyed face to the world. He put the truck into gear, released the brake, and rolled away, listening to an exhaust tick in his engine that he had not previously noticed.

Michael stopped in Laramie outside a pawn shop to use a pay telephone. First he checked the answering machine at what used to be his home, noting with some disappointment that his action betrayed a failure to completely disengage. That failure was underscored by his feeling of deflation on not finding any messages. He placed a second call to his agent in Santa Fe.

"Hello, Gloria," Michael said. "I'm on the road and I can't be reached for a while."

"What's the matter now?" Gloria asked.

Michael imagined the stout woman sitting in the overstuffed chair in front of her television. "Nothing's the matter. My wife is having her pimples cured by the handsome Dr. Bob; I've left the house; and I burned all the new paintings."

"You didn't."

"I did. Like I said. I can't be reached. I'll call you soon. I never loved her anyway."

"When you loved her, you became despondent and tried to kill yourself. Now, you claim you never loved her and so you destroy your work."

The head of the *Dicotyles tajacu* was wrapped in newspaper, sitting on the seat of the truck, dead for twenty-five years, but still breathing. Michael could hear it. He left the boar while he went into the deli near the train tracks for lunch since his stomach was complaining and feeling tight. He sat alone, undisturbed, and ate a vegetarian sandwich from which he pulled out the cucumbers and heard the waitress say, "I don't like those either."

Outside, the air had turned crisp and Michael found himself stepping quickly toward his truck. He was struck suddenly by the distance, not the physical distance, not the miles, nor the change in landscape, but the remoteness from the life he had known just a few days before. He was still a painter: he could buy oils and brushes and canvas and make pictures and there were paintings in the world bearing his mark, but he was no longer a husband, no longer a lover, and he no longer resided in that house in Denver with the detached studio and pool he never wanted.

"Michael?" the voice found him just as he was opening the door of his truck.

Michael turned around. It was Harley Timmons, a sculptor who lived in Laramie, who worked in steel and found objects, who by all measures, in Michael's thinking, was severely untalented, although not unsuccessful. Harley was a heavy man, brawny from lifting steel and working with welding equipment. He had wide-set eyes and an extremely narrow and large nose, which looked like a fin on his face.

"Michael Lawson," Harley said. "I don't believe it. I saw the truck and I said, hey, that looks familiar, then I saw this black guy getting in it and I said, hey, that must be, and it is. How are you doing?"

"Oh, I'm fine," Michael said. "How are you, Harley?"

"Great." Harley pumped Michael's hand and showed big muscular teeth. "I'm just great. What brings you up here?"

"Came up to do a little camping and fishing," Michael said, noting as the last word was out, that he had no camping and fishing gear in his truck. "Headed up to the Winds."

Harley nodded, still flexing his smile. "Why don't you spend the night here and have dinner with Sumiko and me?"

"I don't know."

"I insist. We've got a new guest room we haven't tried out on anyone yet. Come on. You can tell me about the new work." Harley's face seemed so close.

Michael fell back, if not physically, inside. New work? The prospect of discussing the nonexistent was just depressing enough to sound intriguing, he thought. He said, "Okay."

"Well, great, just great," Harley said. "I'm sure there's stuff you've got to do, so I'll just tell you that dinner's at seven, but come anytime you want."

"Thanks."

"Great."

"Great," Michael said. He watched Harley walk away and disappear into the Whole Earth Grain Store in front of which a young woman in a peasant dress swept an already tidy sidewalk.

Michael got into his truck, agreeing with Harley that he probably had some things to do, like maybe buying some camping gear or a fishing rod. That's what he did. He went to a sporting goods store and bought a sleeping bag, a backpack, a campstove, a couple of bottles of white gas, a small tent, a canteen, a four-piece pack fly rod, a reel, two fly boxes, and an assortment of flies, stoneflies, Woolly Buggers, Royal Coachmen, Zug Bugs, sizes 8 to 12, and a fishing license. His bill came to 418 dollars and 47 cents. He paid with his American Express card and a young man helped him carry his new stuff to his truck.

After he bought all of this gear, Michael was eager to get on the road and do some camping; he felt an excitement he hadn't felt in years. But he had told great big Harley that he would be there and, although Harley was not important to Michael, it would be impolite not to show up and awkward trying to explain why he was leaving Laramie just late enough to find a campsite in the dark of night. Michael drove out Ninth Street and into the canyon north of town where he pulled off onto a side road, sat in the back of his truck, and sorted the flies into the compartments of the fly boxes. He classified them slowly, by kind and size, and paid careful attention to their placement.

He left for Harley's house just as the sun was nearing the top of the Snowy Range. He drove into Laramie on Ninth, then turned left on Grand Avenue over to Seventh where in 1913 or so a black man had been lynched on a pole that was still standing, now shouldering power and phone lines. The man had been dragged out of jail by citizens who were chastised the next day by the editor of the town paper for being such poor shots. Out of the hundreds of rounds fired at the hanging man only one bullet found its mark. Michael always looked at the pole as he drove by; the cracked and weathered brown pole pressed against the sky, which tonight was washed lavender at sundown.

At the door of the sizable, but modest house, Michael was met by Sumiko who was as small as Harley was large. Her smile was no less brutish or feral, in fact it was even more savage, coming like an ambush from this little creature.

"It's great to see you," Sumiko said, as her little feet somehow got her behind him. She pushed him into the house, into the vestibule floored with tiles that had been carved by hand, a fish here, a primitive bison there. Michael felt the unevenness of the floor through his shoes. He put down his suitcase.

"It's good to see you, too, Sumiko."

"Harley's not back yet. He's at the chiropractor. He's got a bad back. You know, all that lifting."

Michael nodded.

"Come on into the kitchen," Sumiko said. "You can keep me company while I finish dinner. This is great."

He followed Sumiko through the living room, walking past one of his early paintings. He realized that he had made it, but didn't know how he could have.

"We move that piece around the house," Sumiko said. "I liked it when you used more form."

Michael smiled and hoped she heard.

In the kitchen, Michael found the light white and harsh, discharging from broad panels implanted in the ceiling and ricocheting mercilessly off stainless steel cabinets, stove, and refrigerator.

"What do you think of our new kitchen?" she asked.

"It's very . . . metal," Michael said.

"We like to think so." Sumiko walked to the stove and looked into something she had simmering on a burner. "Sit down, sit down."

Michael sat at the table and watched her tiny feet carry her from refrigerator to stove to cabinet to refrigerator as she tied on a little apron. "How about some wine?" she asked, suddenly.

"I don't drink."

"I remember not liking that about you." She laughed. "May I get you anything to drink? Juice?"

"I'm okay right now," Michael said.

Sumiko took a bottle of white wine from the refrigerator and poured a glass for herself. "A little wine never hurt anybody, Michael."

Michael nodded.

"So, how's Gail?"

"I think she's well," he said.

Sumiko looked at him over the rim of her wine glass. "You think?"

"We're trying out a separation."

"Here's to a successful one," Sumiko said, raising her glass, then taking a sip. "I never liked her anyway. She's not strong enough for you."

"What's in the pot?" Michael asked.

"Oh, it's cream of eggplant soup." She rose to her toes to catch a glimpse of the activity in the pot. "It's the first time I've made it. You're a guinea pig, I guess."

"I'm willing," he said.

Then Sumiko's face changed, she sighed, and her eyes, although not really softening, showed that they wanted to soften, and she walked to Michael and touched his face. "I'm so sorry. Poor, poor Michael," she said, sitting at the table with him. "But isn't this great? Sitting here, together and all."

Michael nodded.

Harley came in through the front door, and said with his booming, smiling voice, "Some fool left a fortune of camping gear outside free for the taking."

Michael stood up as Harley entered the kitchen. "Maybe that's not a good idea," he said.

"Oh, don't worry," Harley said. "This is Laramie, not Denver."

Michael sat back down.

Sumiko handed a glass of wine to Harley. "What did he say about your back?"

"Well, he cracked it this way and he cracked it that way," Harley said, twisting his body to indicate the treatment. "Then he stretched me and told me not to pick up anything heavy. I laughed in his face. I had half a mind to pick him up and laugh right into his face. Like this." He grabbed Sumiko by her waist and she squealed and then he hoisted her to eye level and laughed right in her face and then they laughed together.

"Where's your bathroom?" Michael asked.

"Down the hall," Harley said, letting Sumiko's feet down to the black and white tiles. "You'll see it."

Michael walked down the corridor and before he turned into the bath, he heard Sumiko whisper to Harley, "They've split up." He closed the door behind him and switched on the light, nearly collapsing as he did so: everything was so bright. The room was white everywhere, white fixtures, white walls, white tile, white bidet, white towels, and even the soap in the white dish was white. He wanted to pee just to create some contrast, some relief not merely for his bladder but for his suffering eyes. He was dizzied by the brutal starkness of it all and the headache that had been at work in the back of his brain rose another notch in intensity. He imagined walking into this room and switching on the light in the middle of the night, having just come out of a sound sleep. He might have to do just that. He shuddered as he approximated the magnitude of the headache that might be caused by such a visual concussion. He flushed, washed his hands, reluctantly dried them on a stiff white towel, and went back to Harley and Sumiko in the kitchen.

"Do you have another bathroom?" Michael asked.

"There's one in our bedroom," Harley said, his big smile filled with concern. "Something wrong with the other one?"

"No, nothing," Michael said. "Just wondering. Your house is done very nicely."

"Thanks," Harley said.

"Taste this," Sumiko said, coming to Harley with a spoon, her free hand cupped under it. "Be careful, now, this is hot. Blow on it first." She blew on it for him.

Harley blew on it too, then sucked in the soup. "That's great."

"Want a taste, Michael?" Sumiko asked.

Michael sat down at the table again. "Thanks, but I think I'll wait." He squinted against the pain in his head.

"Something wrong?" Sumiko asked. "You're squinting. Is the light hurting your eyes?"

"Nope."

"Hey, man, you want to lie down before dinner?" Harley asked, sitting across the table, crossing his legs, and playing with the laces of one of his enormous boots.

Michael shook his head.

The doorbell rang. "That'll be Eddie and Simon," Harley said and left the room.

"You'll love these people," Sumiko said. "Eddie's a writer and Simon, he's a doctor and well, you'll see."

Harley came rolling into the kitchen with the guests who were laughing loudly with him. "Michael," Harley said, "Edwina Johns and Simon Seys."

Simon belched out an even louder laugh. "That's really my name," he said to Michael. "Can you believe my parents named me that? I'm just lucky they didn't name me Yadont."

Michael squeezed a smile into the chorus of guffaws. "I'm pleased to meet you," he said.

"I like your paintings," Eddie said abruptly, sitting in the chair that had been Harley's. She looked at Michael's eyes, seeming to get too close, yet they were separated by the table. "Your paintings remind me of my work."

"Sumiko tells me you're a writer," Michael said.

"Yes." She was not laughing now, but looking at Michael with a serious expression.

Michael looked to Simon. "What do you do, Simon?"

"I'm a physician," Simon said. "A dermatologist. I just thought I'd squeeze that in." He laughed again and the rest laughed with him.

"Are you two from Laramie?" Michael asked.

"No, we're from Denver," Eddie said, serious once more.

Michael's heart sank at hearing the word Denver and the word dermatologist together. He figured that all skin doctors in Denver must know one another. Simon must know Bob and therefore, these two people, if not all four of them, were probably all too familiar with the details of Michael's private life.

"Where do you live?" Eddie asked, accepting the glass of wine Harley handed her, but keeping her eyes on Michael.

"I'm kind of floating these days," he said.

"Floating," Simon said and he lifted his arms like a ballerina and pretended to float about the kitchen. "I'm floating. I'm a feather on the wind."

Sumiko danced with him.

"I'm too big to float," Harley said.

Eddie still studied Michael, sipped her wine. "That's what I try to express in my writing. That floating." She put down her glass and gestured, making circles with her limp hands.

Michael nodded to her as if he understood and that made her smile at him. He watched her trace the rim of her glass with her finger.

"You should have seen the rain we drove through on the way up here," Eddie said, breaking away from Michael.

"Not just rain," Simon said, starting to break into a chuckle again. "It was hail getting here."

"Hail?" Sumiko said.

"Not bad," Eddie said.

"The hail you say," said Simon.

Harley's and Sumiko's laughter had wound down into smiles and Michael could sense that Eddie was irritated.

"Why is it," Simon asked, "that hail is always the size of grapefruit or baseballs and never the size of hail?" He laughed more softly, his sounds twisting into the rather sad silence that had come over the room.

"Let's eat," Sumiko said.

"By all means," Eddie said.

Harley and Sumiko expertly herded their guests into the dining room. A glass-topped table stood on an expanse of tan carpet, the wrought-iron legs curved down and back under, and pressed into the nap of the wool. Harley sat Michael beside Eddie with their backs to the wall farthest from the door to the kitchen. Simon sat opposite them. Harley and Sumiko sat at each end of the oval.

The soup was good, Michael thought, but then he was terribly hungry and the taste of anything would have served as a distraction from his headache. He could still see and feel the white light of the bathroom.

"So, how's the skin trade?" Harley asked Simon.

"Very good," Eddie said.

"Oh, he's been waiting to use that all week," Sumiko said. "So, it's not as spontaneous as he would have you believe."

"Put in my place again," Harley said, sounding a little irritated.

Michael felt his mouth opening. He was talking only because, as a guest, he was supposed to say something at some point and he said, "I'd call that Dylan off the bottom."

Eddie, Simon, Harley, and Sumiko looked at him without speaking. They seemed puzzled.

Michael felt compelled to explain. "Dylan Thomas wrote *Adventures in the Skin Trade*."

"Oh, yes," Eddie said.

Everyone laughed.

Eddie looked at Michael with her serious face again and held his eyes just a second too long.

"So how is business?" Harley put the question to Simon once more.

"Breaking out all over," Simon said and laughed.

Harley chuckled politely. Eddie shifted in her chair. Sumiko sipped her wine.

"Business is good," Simon said.

"How's the writing?" Harley asked Eddie.

"I have a story coming out next month. A little journal out of Seattle."

"Great." Harley or Sumiko.

"What kind of things do you write?" Michael asked. "Or is that a stupid question to ask a writer?"

"I'm more interested in tonal columns and color than story," Eddie said. "I'm into texture and contexture. I'm interested in the way opposites fit together, the way they interlock." She took a sip of wine and licked the corners of her lips.

Michael nodded and looked at the others.

"I love your work," Sumiko said to Eddie.

"How do you think of your art?" Eddie asked Michael. "What are you exploring these days?"

"Same as always," Michael said. "I like colors. Sometimes I like yellows. Sometimes blues."

They ate without speaking for a while. The only sounds were the soft dipping of spoons into puddles of cream of eggplant soup, the parting of soup-moistened lips, the clinking of spoon handles against the rims of bowls. The sounds grew louder and louder in Michael's head, especially the smacking of Eddie's lips as she sneaked glances at him.

"You know," Michael said, "I've got a long drive tomorrow and I've got to leave early. So, as good as this is, I've got to get to bed."

"That's okay, Michael," Harley stood, put his napkin on the table. "I'll show you where you're bedding down."

"If you'll all excuse me," Michael said. "Thanks for dinner, Sumiko. It was really good."

"Good night, Michael," Sumiko said.

"It was a pleasure meeting you two," he said to the other guests.

"Same here," Simon said, standing and shaking Michael's hand.

"Maybe I'll see you all in the morning," Michael said.

Eddie gave him one last ogle before he followed Harley, who was saying, "I already grabbed your bag." They walked down the hallway, past the bathroom of monochrome torture and into a small den.

"I forgot Eddie and Simon were staying over, so we've got to put you on this sofa," Harley said.

"Fine with me." Michael looked around the room, at the short couch on which he would be sleeping, at the blond wood paneling, at the green carpet.

"This is the room we haven't done yet," Harley said, apologetically. "The television works if you want to use it."

"Thanks."

"Well, we're at the end of the hall if you need anything."

"Okay."

Harley left Michael and closed the door. Michael sat on the sofa, ran his hand across the scratchy fabric, and leaned his head back.

The far-off chatter and laughter interspersed with an occasional booming "great" was gone. Michael assumed that they had all gone to bed. He uncoiled himself from the sofa and went to the door to listen. Nothing. He had to relieve himself, but he refused to go back to that white bathroom. Although he believed that even without knowing the layout well enough he might do all right in the dark, the room just flat out scared him; his head hurt simply considering it; his stomach tightened into a knot, which, given his present condition, was an unfortunate circumstance. He felt irrational, but hell, being irrational was the least of his worries. Being irrational didn't hurt and didn't poke like pins into the backs of his eyeballs. No, he couldn't go in there. At the front door, however, he was shocked to find that, even though this was "Laramie, not Denver," there was an alarm system. A green light flashed, but Michael didn't know what it meant, whether it was armed or off. He dared not open the door for fear of waking the whole house and maybe summoning every deputy in the territory—cowboys bored shitless at coffee shops just waiting to speed over and point their hair-trigger pistols at him while he squatted next to the holly bush.

He went back and stood in the hallway outside the bathroom. He felt the already piercing pain in his head and was truly afraid of what the light in that room would do to him. He would open the door, flip the switch, and his brain would rupture. If only the room had a window, then at least there might be a small amount of moonlight from outside. He couldn't bring himself to use the room with the door open, because of the obvious potential for interruption and embarrassment. He hadn't liked the feeling he'd gotten from Eddie at dinner, the way she licked her lips even when she wasn't licking her lips, so he was particularly sensitive to the possibility of her finding him in a compromising position. Down at the end of the corridor was the door to Harley and Sumiko's room and in there was another bathroom. It occurred to him that there might be a flashlight in the kitchen. He believed that everyone had one of those messy drawers with rubber bands, pliers, empty matchbooks, and maybe, just maybe a flashlight. He went into the kitchen and prowled about using the moon through the windows, finding the flatware and a drawer full of corkscrews, and finally their equivalent to his junk drawer, but it seemed frighteningly neat and was, after all, without a flashlight. As sometimes happens when one is engaged to the point of distraction, the urge to go suddenly disappeared. Michael decided to return to his room, close his eyes, and consider his predicament. He went back and put himself on the sofa only to find a leg already stretched across it. He jumped up and hit the switch for the overhead fixture. It was Eddie.

"What are you doing in here?" Michael asked.

"I couldn't sleep," she said. She was wearing a gown made of flannel.

"You shouldn't be in here. What if Simon wakes up? What if he were to come in here? What would he say seeing you sitting there like that?"

"Who cares what Simon says?"

"Well, Simon didn't say you could come in here." Michael felt silly saying that. "Is that really his name?"

Eddie nodded, sitting up and leaning toward him. "Sumiko said you tried to kill yourself."

"What?"

"She said you ate paint." Eddie swallowed. "I love the passion of that."

"I see." He walked over and sat beside her on the sofa. "I did eat paint, but I didn't try to kill myself. I'm just a dumb shit. Now, I don't know what kind of romantic picture you've concocted of me, nor what kind of game you've conjured up for us to play, but I'm not going to be a part of it."

"You haven't heard what I have in mind," she said.

"I don't need to hear it." Michael's brains pushed at the walls of his cranium. "I really think you should go on back to your room, okay?"

"A kiss first."

"No."

"Just one," she said, pouting. "I'm good at it."

"I'm sure." Michael sighed. "Please?"

Eddie stood and slinked across the room toward the door, trying to achieve a seductive look in her flannel nightshirt. "I'm going," she said.

Michael looked at her feet. They were enormous.

"Good night, Michael."

When she was gone and his door was closed, he shut his eyes and pushed out a breath. His stomach began to hurt and he felt pressure again to find a toilet. There was no putting it off this time; he'd have to suffer the consequences of using the white room. He went out into the hall only to find the door closed and a stripe of light at the threshold. Eddie was in there doing god-knew-what and he didn't dare knock and make it look as if he were coming after her. His stomach did a flip. He was in pain and in a hurry.

He made his way down the hall to his hosts' bedroom door. He turned the knob slowly and pushed into the room. He could hear breathing. The darkness of his room and the hallway had helped his eyes adjust and with his pupils all dilated he was able to see around the bedroom by the light from outside. He saw what must have been the bathroom door and treaded softly toward it. About halfway across the room, he realized that the breathing he was hearing sounded a certain way. He then heard Sumiko's small voice cooing, "Oh, my big steel baby," and Michael thought he was going to die. He got into the bathroom and felt around on the wall for the light switch, then closed the door before throwing it. Pain detonated in his head like a blasting cap and the heat of it ripped through his eyes. This room turned out to be just as bright white as the other one. He was reeling and losing his balance, but he had a reason for being there and he managed to drop his trousers and sit on the toilet, covering his eyes with his hands.

Finished, Michael automatically reached back and flushed and immediately cringed at the subsequent noise. The tank filled and he listened at the door, learning that Harley and Sumiko hadn't heard the plumbing because of their involvement. He tried not to focus on their sounds, but couldn't help hearing them since his headaches always heightened his auditory capacity. He switched off the light, sat on the floor, and realized that when they were done, one of them would probably be headed his way.

Michael crawled across the floor to the tub and climbed into it. He pushed his back up against the cool enamel and waited, trying to think and not think at the same time. What was it with these windowless bathrooms? He froze at the sound of the door opening and closed his eyes, anticipating the light being turned on, but no switch was thrown and the room remained dark. A mere twelve inches and the shower curtain separated him from whom he was sure was Sumiko sitting on the toilet urinating; the sound was just like Gail's. She even pulled paper off the roll before she was done like Gail. Michael's heart was racing, but strangely his headache was letting up—yet another bit of evidence against the theory that his symptoms were stress-related. Sumiko finished, yawned, flushed, and left the room with the door open.

Several minutes dragged by and Michael thought he could hear Harley's snoring. He pulled himself out of the tub and crawled across the icy tiles to the door, where he paused and satisfied himself that, indeed, Harley was snoring. He stayed on his hands and knees as he moved across the carpet of the bedroom and bumped into someone.

"I've been searching all over for you," Eddie said.

Michael felt faint.

A light came on and the very first thing Michael saw was Eddie's gangly and naked body on hands and knees right in front of him.

"What in the hell is going on?" yelled Harley who was sitting up in bed.

Michael stood up quickly, looking in horror at Eddie and then at Harley and finally Sumiko. Sumiko had the covers pulled up to her neck, but Harley was now standing, butt-naked beside the bed. Michael saw the man's little penis and looked away, but what he confronted were naked Eddie's enormous feet. Michael wanted to scream, but nothing rose from his throat, although a scream would have served as an appropriate and suitable accompaniment to the way he tore out of there.

Michael ran to the den, grabbed his shoes, jacket, and bag and bumped into Simon, who was coming out of the guest room into the hallway. Again, Michael wanted to let out some unintelligible shrill bellow and again his lungs failed him. He ran away from Simon, who stood confused and uncharacteristically silent in his red flannel pajamas. He reached the front door, turned the lock, and set off the loudest alarm he'd ever heard, a screeching horn that penetrated his head. In the background he could hear Harley say, "What in hell is going on here?!" and Simon say, "Edwina!" Michael ran to his truck, fumbled with his keys, got the engine started, and drove off as the lights of neighbors' houses began to snap on. He looked over to find the head of the *Dicotyles tajacu* still on the seat beside him, still neatly wrapped.

Michael drove north out of Laramie into stiff and increasingly frigid wind. He thought of the fire that had consumed his recent work, recalled the odor of the burning oil-covered canvases. The Virginian Hotel in Medicine Bow was dark, lonely, and most significantly, closed when he arrived there at three in the morning. He bundled up in his new sleeping bag and huddled up against the wall out of the wind. In the morning when the doors opened, he would sit down and order the mediocre breakfast fare for which the hotel was regionally famous and then continue north for the Big Horns where he would camp, fish, and probably freeze. He thought about the head of the *Dicotyles tajacu* on the passenger seat of his truck and wished it were alive; alive, so that he could let it go, watch it trot off on short, sturdy legs across the prairie. But it had no legs, it was just the severed head with a hole where an eye had been, and a fake eye at that, seeing nothing even in its newest, most firmly inserted condition. The head was only a head.

Pissing on Snakes

Laney decided to walk the remaining miles to the shitty little desert town where the shitty little police had her shitty little brother locked in a cell for drinking too much and generally being himself. She was walking because the belt on the water pump of her truck's engine had broken. Mitch walked alongside her and his mouth was, as usual, open:

"I told you not to buy a piece of shit Japanese truck."

Laney was a couple of yards ahead of him and she muttered, "Fuck you, you lame-ass rodeo has-been."

"What was that?"

"I said, 'fuck you.'" She stopped and turned to him, looking at his narrow face.

"And what else?"

"I think 'fuck you' about says it all."

"You know, I didn't have to come with you."

She laughed and again with her back to him said, "I didn't ask you to come. I told you to stay. I didn't ask you to walk to town with me either. You can go back now if you want." In her pocket she fumbled with the string she had used to measure the pump belt.

Mitch caught up with her, matched stride with her.

She looked over at him. He wasn't a bad-looking idiot, but an idiot nonetheless and it was laughable that he considered himself to be tagging along as protection. She wasn't sure why she had first gone out with him, much less why she had agreed to let him come along now while she bailed out her good-for-nothing brother.

"Laney, I'm sorry. Okay?"

"Sorry for what?"

Mitch looked down at his sneakers hitting the highway. "I don't know, but I am. I don't want to fight, that's all. I'm really tired of the fighting."

"Then take your stupid ass back to the truck and wait there."

"Why do you talk like that?"

"I'm not talking like anything. Why do you hear like that?"

"Like a damn sailor."

"Fuck you."

"See," Mitch said.

She glanced at him quickly, then looked back at the highway. He was too tall and too skinny and his hair was retreating, showing more of his face, a face not aging well. His mustache at least worked as cover. She took a deep breath. "Okay," she said, "no more fighting."

Mitch nodded. He looked behind them. "You'd think one car would go by." He kicked his heels as he walked. "Your brother has a drinking problem."

"He's a low-life scum. Of course he has a drinking problem. But he's my brother." She sighed and rolled her head to loosen her neck. "Whatever the hell that means."

"Can't choose your family," Mitch said.

"That's true up to a point," she said.

"What's that supposed to mean?"

"Figure it out."

The sun was on full and Laney was sweating. The dry air was stealing away the moisture and any possibility of coolness. She was thirsty. "I wish I'd brought a canteen."

"Yeah, me too," Mitch said, then, "I mean, I wish I'd brought one, too."

"Christ, Mitch, calm down." Laney couldn't believe she had

ever let this guy touch her. It wouldn't happen again, she assured herself.

The service station was one of those no-name kind with a gravel yard. The pumps were old and dusty. It was still several miles to the town, so Laney hoped it would have the belt she needed.

No one came out as they approached the station and there was no one in the office. Laney parked her face over the water fountain and let the stream wash her forehead. The water was barely cool, but it felt good. She drank slowly, then stepped away to allow Mitch a turn. She called out, "Hello!"

Mitch stood, wiping his mouth with the back of his hand. "Nobody home?"

Laney observed the belts on the far wall, narrow loops of black wrapped midlength with paper and hung on hooks. She pulled the circle of string from her pocket. "At least I can find out if they have what I need."

Mitch stepped through the open door into the garage.

Laney pulled down a couple of belts and compared them to the loop of string. One was close enough that she believed it would work. She called to Mitch.

"What?" He stepped back into the office. "Find it?"

"I think so."

"Good."

"You didn't find the attendant? Did you check the rest room?"

"No rest room," Mitch said.

"There's got to be one." Laney looked at the belt in her hand. "This thing doesn't have a price on it."

"Can't be more than ten bucks."

Laney frowned at Mitch. "Well, I'm not leaving ten bucks if the damn thing only costs three ninety-five. Did you look around back?"

"Yeah, I checked during an out-of-body experience," Mitch said.

"You don't have to be a snot."

Laney led the way out and around the broken-down building, pausing to look across the desert in the direction of town. Behind the station was a door marked "Wash." Laney knocked and fell back a step.

"Go on inside," she said to Mitch.

Mitch looked at her.

"In case he's in the middle of something."

"I don't want to see him if he is," Mitch said.

"Go on. Don't be a baby."

Mitch opened the door, leaned inside a bit, and came back. "Oh, fuck," he said.

"What is it?" Laney moved forward to the doorway and saw the red-covered floor. "God. Is that blood?"

"Yeah, I'm pretty sure." Mitch turned away and let the door close.

Laney looked all around, feeling dizzy, her heart racing. She studied two derelict cars some yards away in the sage. Mitch was looking around, too.

"It's a gas station rest room," he said. "The blood doesn't mean a thing."

Laney and Mitch went back to the front of the station and into the office. A lizard on the counter startled Laney. It was then that she noticed the blood on the floor behind the desk.

"Mitch, look here."

Mitch did and shook his head. "This is bad. We'd better call the cops."

Laney reached for the phone and listened for a tone. She looked at Mitch and shook her head. She watched Mitch run out across the yard, past the pumps to the phone booth. He held the receiver and severed cord in the air for Laney to see before throwing it to the ground.

Laney felt exposed. Mitch walked back to her.

"What do you think?" he asked.

Laney looked at the pump belt still clutched in her fist. "We can go back and get the truck, then drive to town for the police or we can just walk to town from here. Same amount of time. Probably take longer to go to the truck and put this thing on."

Mitch looked at the road. "I'm not sure about walking out there either way, you know?"

"It's one or the other, Mitch. We can't just stay here."

"Shit."

Laney went to the fountain and drank more water. "I say we go back to the truck."

"Why?"

She shrugged and thought for a while, looking at the road. "No cars passed us either way. So they must have gone in the direction of town."

Mitch nodded. "Yeah, that sounds right. Okay, let's get going then."

Laney drank more water, drank until she was full. She licked her lips and said, "I suggest you drink some more, too."

Mitch did.

They started walking back in the direction of Laney's truck. Laney became aware again of the belt in her hand. She considered hiding it under her shirt. If there were a crook or killer and he drove by and saw it, he'd know she'd been to the station. She was also troubled by the fact that technically the belt was stolen. What if the police found them and decided they had something to do with whatever the hell had happened at the station? She carried the belt close to her side and away from the road. The rubber was slimy against her sweating palm.

A big brown Oldsmobile came toward them on its way to town. Laney waved for the car to stop, but the elderly couple tightened visibly, swerved to the other lane, and kept going at an increased clip. The idea of being blamed for some crime seemed less far-fetched as she imagined the old couple finding the blood in the wash room. She walked faster.

"I don't like this," Mitch said, sounding close to tears.

Laney decided she hated Mitch and she hated herself for being with him, for allowing him to be with her. So, he had rid-den a bull. Big deal. Besides, he had been thrown before the gate was fully open. Trying not to think about the present situation, though, she spoke to him, "Mitch, what do you want to do with your life?"

He was silent for a few seconds. "I don't know." Then he smiled. "Drink beer and get lucky."

"You know," she said, "somewhere there's a twit with half a brain and big tits who would think that's funny. And between the two of you, you'd have half a brain."

"Fuck you."

"You wish."

"Hey, you know, this stuff ain't my fault."

Laney shook her head. He was right; it wasn't his fault. But that didn't make him any less despicable and sad, it didn't make him any less like the string of duds Laney had found herself with in recent years.

"This is your fucking brother's fault," Mitch said.

"Shut up."

"If the little asshole hadn't run off and gotten drunk, then . . ."

"And if your father hadn't poked your mother," Laney said and then was sorry she'd said it.

"That's the mouth I'm talking about," Mitch whined.

"Sorry," Laney said.

They walked on another forty or fifty yards.

"It's no big deal," he said. "We just put that belt on and drive to town and tell the cops what we saw. That's all there is to it."

"Okay." A chill ran through her.

Mitch reached for her hand.

"Don't touch me."

Laney heard the car coming up behind them, a loud engine in need of a muffler. It came from the direction of town and slowed as it approached. She was afraid to look back, but afraid not to look. If it was the police she didn't want to appear guilty. She was confused by the fact that she felt guilty. She glanced back and saw a rusty yellow mid-seventies LeMans. A man with long blond hair was driving and a man with a shaved head was trying to lean out of the partially lowered rear window. She saw that Mitch was looking at them, too.

"Don't look at them," Laney muttered.

Mitch looked forward as they kept walking.

The car was now beside them, matching their walking speed. Laney looked again.

"Gotta problem?" the driver asked, leaning out of his window, his free arm hanging down loose, his hand seeming to be mere inches from the pavement.

"No, no problem," Mitch said.

"Why you walking?" the driver asked.

"Yeah, why you walking?" the bald man in the back seat echoed.

Laney and Mitch kept walking. "Just walking," Laney said. She tried to hide the pump belt against her side.

"Just walking," said the man in the back seat, laughing. Laney didn't look, but imagined him bouncing up and down. Bouncing up and down just like her brother did when he was with his rowdy friends. Thinking of her brother in connection with these thugs made her feel bad, then more frightened.

The car rolled a few yards ahead of them and Laney saw the man sitting beside the driver for the first time. His face was buried in a dirty red beard.

"You married?" the driver asked.

Laney stopped and looked right at them. "Just leave us the hell alone." She remembered the belt and tried to conceal it.

The men hooted.

"Yeah, we're married," Mitch said.

"You're a lucky man," the driver said. "Where you walking to? Want a ride? We'll give you a ride."

"No, no, thanks," Mitch said, "our truck is just down the road a ways."

"Okay, then." The LeMans drove on, and the bald man kept looking at them through the back window.

Laney watched the car disappear down the road and then hit Mitch with the pump belt as hard as she could across his back and shoulder. He ran away some steps.

"What?"

"If you had even a piece of a brain, you'd be dangerous," Laney said.

"I got rid of them," he said.

"Where do you think they're going? They're going to my truck."

"You don't know that."

Laney walked away from the road out across the desert.

"What are you doing?" Mitch asked.

"You go on to the truck. Here, take the fucking belt." She tossed it to him. "And here are the fucking keys."

He stopped her with a raised hand before she tossed those, too. "Calm down. Where are you going?"

"I'm going to town. I'm going to get off this shit highway and walk out there where they can't see me." She turned and marched quickly through the sage and over the prickly pears. She was glad to be walking on ground instead of pavement.

Mitch caught up and walked beside her.

They walked east and down into a dry river bed, and followed that north. Laney was glad she had drunk so much water. The sun was intense and robbing her of energy. She wanted to keep all of her fluids, but the pressure in her bladder grew worse. She considered that being scared was exacerbating the problem. She walked away from the bed toward a stand of rocks.

"Where you going?" Mitch asked.

"I'm going to take a piss, okay?" Laney rounded the rocks and stepped onto a large downward-sloping stone flat, out of sight of Mitch. She pulled down her jeans and underwear and squatted over the rock. She closed her eyes and waited, taking a deep breath, trying to relax. She heard a sound beside her, opened her eyes, and found a stream striking the rock just ahead of her and to her left. Mitch was standing beside her, urinating. Laney shook her head.

"Jesus Christ," she said. "I can't even pee by myself."

Mitch sighed.

Laney quickly pulled up her clothes before letting out a drop and walked away, fastening her pants. As she stepped from the rock to the ground something caught her eye. A sunning diamondback was only three feet from her. The dull sand color of the snake stung her senses. She hadn't disturbed it, so there was no rattling, no acknowledgment of her presence, but still it took her breath away. She looked across the rock flat and saw that there were snakes everywhere. She looked back and realized that she had absently wandered into the middle of a nest of basking rattlers. The sight and the thought that she had been in the middle of them made her shiver for a second.

"What is it?" Mitch asked, noticing her distress. Then he looked to where she was looking. "God almighty," he said softly. "Fuck," he said louder. "Look at all these fuckers!"

Laney stepped back some more, leaving Mitch alone in the middle of all the rattlers.

"Look at this shit," Mitch said.

Laney looked at Mitch and wanted to laugh. She turned and started to walk away.

"Where are you going?" he asked.

"Town."

"Wait. How did you get over there? How'd you get past these snakes? How'd you do that?"

Laney answered him without looking back. "I'm used to it."

Wash

Dusk came on and the pinacate bugs were out of their holes, and trudging along the sand wash. Lucien Bradley pushed his toe into the path of one of the large beetles and watched it stand on its head. He glanced up at the shriek of a chat-little and noticed the pink in the sky. Although it didn't show promise of rain, he walked up to the high ground near his truck to settle in for the night. He remembered how quickly desert floods could occur, how his father would not drive across a dip in the road if there was water standing in its trough. The chill of evening was already upon him, pushing his shoulders tight into his body and his palms flat together. He built a fire, ate a sandwich that he had bought some miles back outside of Las Cruces, and then rolled out his sleeping bag. He warmed his hands before the flame one last time and arranged sticks by the fire before slipping into his sleeping bag. Lying under the moon he noticed a saguaro cactus standing beyond the glow of his fire. He tried to recall the last time he had been able to sleep in the desert. The desert he and his father had shared was not like this one. The high desert was not as severe, not as frightening, constant, relentless. It was harsh only for its lack of water. His father spoke to him, a dead voice in the wind. He told Lucien what a fool he was, a fool to love the low land, a fool to have left school and joined the army, a fool to have no answers, and a fool to expect answers to questions he was foolish enough to ask. "I'm dead now, you fool," his father said, "and I've died to fucking spite you. Giving up life for what?" Lucien put a stick on the fire and said, "Fuck you, too." And then he felt stupid for talking aloud to his father. The dead made for decent memories, but lousy conversation. Fire was the substance of stuff, he thought, heat and consumption, light and vacuum, the center of power and the edge of approach and all the kinds of philosophical shit his father used to say about it. He was tempted to shove his hand into the flames.

His mother would be waiting in Taos for him and she wouldn't tell him to get fucked. She would hug him like he was no fool, cry about his father's death, and smile over her son's homecoming. She would ask him to tell her about Honduras and then not listen. He laughed as he thought about the low desert surrounding him, thinking about water, no water. But when the water came it meant death. Mice and snakes and nests and anything else would be swept away by flooding, sudden rivers on a timeless landscape. To drown in a desert, that was the way to die, sinuses replete with sandy water, dead eye to dead eye with rattlers in the flow. Lucien closed his eyes and thanked God or something, anything, that he was out of the army, lost, but out of the army, no smarter, but out of the army.

The morning came to him along with thoughts of fishing and tying flies. The close work with the feathers, thread, and fur had always relaxed him. He drove the two hours north to Albuquerque and decided not to stop, not to eat. He decided to make his mother happy by arriving at her house famished. Her house—he replayed the words and they sounded right—her house. It was not his home; it hadn't been for some time. It was a hard thought, but he wondered if he needed his mother. He loved her, but did he need her? A referee was of little use in a ring with one fighter, but had there ever been a fight, or was he kicking himself silly for things he'd never had a chance to say to his father, or worse, had the chance but not the inclination?

Camel Rock was a landmark because big rocks tend to be landmarks. It was a sign that he was closer to his country, but it was a sad sight, the dromedary outcropping crawling with camera-toting visitors and their oily-fingered offspring, nature's new erosive element: people who were shaping land just like time and water and wind, but leaving no beauty, just marks. He noted the rock as he rolled by, but kept his eyes forward on the highway with its steady, mesmerizing, reassuring yellow line. Then he was waiting for the view, the view he would get when he was through the mountain pass and looking down on the Taos Valley, where the Rio Grande Gorge snaked through like gossip.

He reached the vista, stopped his truck, and got out to have a look. It was as he always remembered it, no larger than life, but the biggest life he knew. He was like the space between the walls of the gorge, being from a black father and a white mother. He was not Indian, not Mexican, but he looked like he could be either. The gorge was a vastness that couldn't be ignored, but really couldn't be defined. There were some black people in Santa Fe and certainly in Albuquerque, but not in Taos, save for the occasional counterculture, transplanted, California-style would-be artist passing through or settling to work in a gallery or boutique. A thunderhead formed over the hills to the west as he drove through Ranchos de Taos and he counted another five fast-food joints added to the awful strip that threatened to make even this place, so singular in setting, just another clone row of America, another burb of the interstatic. He drove through downtown Taos and its traffic of beat-up pickups and BMWs and rusty '63 Impalas and Mercedes to El Prado and then down the dirt road that led to his mother's house.

Lucien's mother cried and hugged him and with her small body pulled him into the house. The place looked the same, but it appeared quieter. His mother was a strong woman, a fighter, so the house was still alive, she would never let the house die, but it was quiet. The house was special to Eva, and now it was hers, just hers; her husband was dead but she had her home. Lucien liked the way it felt. He was surprised that he could not feel the presence of his father and more surprised that he wanted to. He knew that if he raised the issue with his mother she would tell him in no uncertain terms that his father was everywhere, breathing in each room, stuck like cobwebs in each corner. So he didn't mention it.

"Food, you need food, don't you?"

"Actually, I'm starving."

"It won't take a minute." She was off to the kitchen; her son trailed behind her. "I wasn't expecting you until tomorrow." Turning to see him again, she said, "You look well. Fit. You look fit."

"I suppose I am fit. But look at you. You look terrific, Ma. Have you been working out, some aerobics or something? Playing a little basketball?"

"I walk. I walk everywhere these days. Except to the grocery store. That's too far away, at least for carrying sacks."

Lucien sat at the table and watched his mother gather food from the refrigerator and cupboards and drop pans on the stove with noise that wasn't noise. "Pancakes, eggs, and sausage. I know it's lunch time, but that's what you need." She hesitated for a moment, twisting her small face. "No eggs. There are eggs in the pancakes. We've got to watch our cholesterol."

"Yes, ma'am." He watched as she broke eggs into a bowl with flour and milk. "You do look really good, Ma."

Without turning to face him, she said, "I feel good. I miss your father, but people die. You live with it." Then quickly, "Tell me about Honduras."

"Nothing to report really. It wasn't much different from Espanola, to tell the truth. Mostly we just sat around the base." He recalled the rocking motion of the soldiers he knew, leaning at sills while reading letters from home, rocking back and forth on their heels, just waiting, waiting to go home, waiting to be told to do something, waiting to be told not to wait any longer. "It was pretty boring. A lot of waiting."

"Your room is all ready for you. It's not exactly how you left it."

"You mean it's clean."

"It's very clean. And let's try to keep it that way." She poured batter onto the skillet.

Lucien listened to the hiss of the frying cakes as he thought about sleeping in the house. He didn't want to stay there, didn't want to shower where his father showered, sit on the same toilet. He realized for the first time that he was afraid of missing the man, afraid of finally facing the loss. Until now it had been convenient to blame his father for his own death, thinking that if he had taken better care, if he had slowed down, if . . . . "I'm not staying here."

Spatula in hand, she turned. "What?"

"I need to find a place of my own," was the best he could come up with.

"Well, I can understand that, but you just got here."

"I'm going to find something as soon as I can. Today maybe." He felt like a kid caught in a stupid lie that was snowballing.

There were no tears from Eva's eyes, no sounds of crying. "That's stupid. And mean." She turned, examined the pancakes, and tossed one into the garbage.

She was right. He didn't want to hurt his mother. "Ma, I've been sleeping in a bunk under a fat guy with gas for five months. I need room."

"You'll have the room to yourself."

"I know." He paused. "It was a long drive. Of course I'll stay here."

She stepped to him and touched his face.

"I'm sorry, I didn't mean to hurt your feelings." He looked about the kitchen. "I'm scared of missing Dad, I guess."

She turned to the cooking and he knew that she was crying.

His father was certainly dead. His tying room, the small room at the back of the house where he had fashioned his flies for fishing, was neat. All of his tools, his vise, his bobbins, bodkins, and scissors were there, but everything was orderly. The feathers that he used were packed away in clear plastic boxes with mothballs, as were the squares of fur: rabbit, deer, elk, bear, muskrat. Lucien sat at the desk, loosened and tightened the vise, and looked at the hooks sitting in plastic cups, smallest to largest, left to right. So much order would have driven his father crazy. When his father was alive, the desk was a mess. There were pieces of feathers floating and clinging to the sleeves of his sweater, the debris of trimmed deer hair everywhere, snippets of thread and floss and tinsel littering the floor. Now it was all neat, arranged as death must be because it is so simple.

He grew up confused by his father's belief in simple and precise answers; one answer in particular, that one can move away and live without the world. Now, Lucien understood all too well why his father moved to the high desert. It was a matter of leaving the world and its problems with his race behind. So he left black people and hopefully white people as well, but "of course there was no escaping them." Lucien resented his father protecting him from the world. He allowed himself to be herded off to college and directed toward his father's profession until finally he "lost his mind" and joined the army. Lucien could not shake the look on his father's face when he received the news of Lucien's enlistment.

Lucien took the cover off of a box of hackle feathers and pulled out a cape of grizzly. He admired the dark and white pattern and imagined the wings of an Adams sticking straight up. It was a good cape, the feathers stiff, varying greatly in size. He put a size 14 hook into the vise and secured it. He threaded black thread through the tube of a bobbin, and made the first turns around the shank. He already felt the tension leaving him. He chose two small grizzly hackle feathers for the wings and tied them perpendicularly to the shank, the motions feeling easier than he imagined they would. It had been so long. He found some brown hackle in the box, tied in a feather of it and another feather of grizzly. He cut a few barbules of brown and grizzly for the tail and tied them down. With each step of building the fly he felt better and he could hear his father's voice, the voice that he loved, not the voice that his aching heart had concocted. From a patch of muskrat hide he teased some hairs and rolled them onto the waxed thread, wrapped the hook, and formed the body. He remembered fighting with his fingers as a young boy trying to do this, these motions that now seemed so simple. He remembered his father behind him, watching, laughing, instructing. Finally he had the last hackle feather gripped in the pliers and was turning it round the fly; the feather was fanning out and pointing in every direction. The lure began to breathe. He had sweet memories of doing this through the winter in anticipation of spring fishing. When he did find a place to live he would take the things that had been his father's and use them, keep them alive.

"Are you okay?" Eva leaned against the doorjamb.

"Yes, ma'am."

"I straightened up in here."

"So I see." Lucien pushed himself away from the desk and stood up, arching his back to loosen it. "It's a lot easier to find things now."

"Tired?"

"It was a long drive. That truck's seat is like a board, too. To tell the truth, I was surprised it even started after sitting for so long."

"At least you didn't have to worry about anybody stealing it."

Lucien laughed. "Yes, it's a sorry-looking critter."

"Why don't you take a nap?"

Lucien nodded, walked to his mother, and embraced her.

"I'll make a trip to the grocery store while you're asleep."

"I'll go when I get up if you like."

In his room, Lucien tossed his bags into the corner. The room was clean, but retained the smell of his childhood: it reminded him of jeans and frogs and board games. He stretched out on the mattress and felt his body give in to its firmness. When he was in high school he sneaked Sarah Begay into his room while his parents were away, but she never surrendered to the comfort of the mattress, nor to Lucien. He remembered her beautiful dark eyes saying no, and he always wanted to thank her because he wasn't ready then either. He was pretty sure that even then she wasn't a virgin. He believed that she had said no because she understood something about life. But apparently she didn't understand enough, because she married out of high school, had three kids before she was nineteen, and looked all of forty at twenty. Still, thinking back, he would have liked to sleep with her.

He recalled the smell of drying chili peppers and the colors of the corn festival dances and he decided that being home felt good. It felt good even if he didn't know how he fit into the landscape.

He remembered the stories his father had told him about finding the side of the pillow that held the good dreams. Even now a bad dream would cause him to turn his pillow over. Once he even exchanged his pillow surreptitiously for another soldier's.

He heard either a raccoon or a coyote disturbing the garbage cans in the backyard. Lucien liked coyotes. They were perhaps the most adaptable of mammals, still roaming parts of Los Angeles. Coyotes were cunning and secretive and inquisitive and social. His father had liked coyotes. The old man had once sneaked back to a roadside zoo with him and released several caged coyotes. Lucien remembered asking, "What if they don't know how to hunt?"

"Then they'll die," his father said as they climbed back into the truck. "But they won't be caged. That's why we live here, Lucien."

The weather of early fall was a reminder of how kind the high desert could be. Life up there was simply too easy, he recalled. It made the people lazy. The laziness was represented in the pots of the Indians from Taos Pueblo. Lucien remembered realizing this fact as a child of ten. He was in the Indian museum down in Albuquerque with his father and mother, standing before a glass case, and there were pots from Zuni, from Cochiti, from Acoma, all beautiful, well-formed, and full of power or love or something scary like that, and then there were the pots from Taos. "Loose," was how his father described the lopsided vessels, but even as a child Lucien could see the disparity. He concluded then, and his growing up there substantiated his thinking, that the things which filled the pots came too easily, and so both, contents and containers, were taken for granted. He watched his friends, white, Mexican, and Indian learn that life was a slow climb up a greased pole with just enough of what you needed at hand to keep you going. The beauty of the place negated the desire to add to the beauty, to give back. Taos was a minefield of galleries, and the so-called artists seemed to be interested in underscoring their names and not in giving back. Canvas after canvas, the same, the same, the same. People came to ski and sun and pay a camera fee at the Pueblo. They came to kick up property values and see their fashionable friends at natural bakeries, came to buy silver and turquoise on the plaza, came to buy art: "Yes, this piece was done by a woman in Arizona. She's interested in the Indian legends. She has a degree in anthropology." But then you looked at the mountains, Lucien thought, and all of those people disappeared. It was where he grew up, this country fat with beauty.

The sun was beginning its decline as Lucien pulled into the lot of the small market just minutes from his mother's house. He was glancing at the list as he entered, feeling for a cart, and was startled when he looked up to find his passage toward the produce section blocked by two men. Manny Archuleta and Rick Gillis stood smiling in front of the cart.

"Soldier boy," Rick said.

"Not anymore." Lucien reached out and shook their hands. "You guys in here for a couple cans of dog food or something?"

"Home for good?" Manny asked, his big face broken with the lopsided Elvis grin that he had cultivated in high school.

"Well, out of the army for good."

"Shoot anybody?" Rick asked.

"Not yet." Lucien pushed the cart past them and toward the produce. "You guys can walk with me, but I've got to get this stuff and get home."

"Looking forward to some home cooking?" Rick plucked a grape from a bunch on a table, popped it into his mouth, and spat the seeds on the floor. A passing woman with a child stared at him.

"You're a real beauty, you know that," Lucien said.

"Sorry about your father," Manny said.

"Thanks. That's the way it goes, I guess." Lucien grabbed a couple of onions.

"What are you doing tonight?" Rick asked.

Lucien laughed. "I'm sitting around the house with my mother. What the hell did you think I'd be doing?"

"After that?"

"Sleeping."

"Nah, come on, go out with us," Manny said. "Like old times."

"I'm kinda beat."

"We'll be at the Blue Corn until late if you change your mind," Rick said. "Okay?"

"Okay."

"Well, all right then."

Lucien watched them leave the store with a handful of grapes each.

He finished shopping, and listened to the Spanish being spoken in the lanes of packaged food. He looked at the brown faces of big-eyed children wanting cookies, wanting to get into carts, wanting to push carts, wanting. He found the ceiling lights of the market harsh.

The clouds of late afternoon were fat and flat-bottomed as if resting on a table of glass. Lucien had not enjoyed his trip to the market. It was good to see his old friends, even though he felt no closeness to them, but after his tour through the aisles he waited in the checkout line behind a woman of high fashion.

He drove the groceries home to his mother, watched her cook for him again, and listened as she told him that his father's illness had come on quickly and that he had suffered only marginally. That was her word, "marginally," and he wondered where she had acquired it and just what it meant. She fed him beef brisket, green beans, and posole.

"I saw Rick and Manny at the market."

His mother nodded, said nothing.

"They look like they're doing okay."

"They work at the lumberyard, both of them." She said it as if it were a bad thing to work at the lumberyard. She had never liked either of them. "All these years at the lumberyard."

"I guess any job around here is a good one."

"I suppose." She drank from her water glass. "That Rick is a strange character, don't you think?" She paused. "Are you going back to school?"

"I don't know, Ma."

"You could wind up where they are."

"I suppose. Working at the lumberyard wouldn't be bad work."

"I guess no work is bad work, but still . . ." She stopped.

They finished eating without saying much of anything. Lucien cleared the table and got ready to wash the dishes.

"That was really good. And just enough, too. I was a little scared you were going to make a lot of food and I wouldn't be able to stop eating."

"Well, I'm trying to establish healthy habits."

"That's good." He turned off the water.

"You know, you're welcome to go out."

"I told them I was spending the evening with my best gal. They asked me to share, but I told them I didn't think they could handle her."

She slapped his rear with the rag she had used to wipe down the table.

"But maybe after you go to bed."

"Okay, honey."

Lucien went through his father's fly boxes while his mother knitted. She told him she was making a sweater for a new baby down the road. She told him three times. The television was on with the sound low. He could see the meaningless motions and facial expressions and just hear the hum of music and canned laughter. He watched his mother's fingers making their sure movements with yarn and was mesmerized. He turned his eyes to the television screen, but didn't see anything, didn't understand anything.

Lucien sat there and felt angry. He didn't understand it and felt in no hurry to understand it. He just felt it. It felt good to feel anything. He wasn't mad at his mother, but as he looked down at the coffee table he knew he could break it in two. His father once told him while they were chopping wood in the backyard that being angry was a part of life. His father had worked up a good sweat and stopped to lean on the axe. "White people don't understand," he said. "Your mother's a good woman, as good a heart as you'll find, but she can't know." Lucien looked at his mother again. He loved her, but she couldn't know. His father had been right, and he couldn't explain it because he didn't know. His father left him with only a vague understanding of his anger, a vague awareness and respect for it. Lucien left the house, but didn't go to the Blue Corn to join his friends. He drove north toward Questa and then across the mountains to Red River. He just drove.

It was well after three when Lucien coasted into the driveway. He shut down the engine a hundred yards away so as not to wake his mother. He was tired, but he didn't want to sleep; he didn't think he could.

Inside, he caught sight of the fly boxes he'd left on the coffee table and decided he'd go fishing. He didn't go to his room for his rod and reel; instead he went to his father's gear. He felt good about using it, knowing that the man would want it used. He chose the four-piece pack rod and the Battenkill reel with double-tapered line. He wore his father's vest and loaded the pockets with a box of terrestrials and another with a bunch of different-sized Royal Wulffs. His father would often fish only one pattern; he insisted that if you presented it correctly a trout would take anything. Lucien put on some coffee and made three cheese and olive sandwiches while it brewed. He poured the coffee into a Thermos, wrote a note to his mother, imagining her smiling as she read it, and left the house quietly. He was sorry he had to start the truck, but his mother would get back to sleep.

It was still dark when Lucien arrived at the parking lot at the head of the trail that led down to the confluence of the Rio Grande and the Red River. It was about a mile hike down the steep path, full of switchbacks, which was easy enough in the light of day, but treacherous in the dark. His light had a good beam though. With it he found the startled eyes of raccoons and other small animals. The trail was still familiar. A couple of deer didn't hear him until he was very close, and they scared him when they jumped and ran down through the junipers. He thought the animals did well to fear him. First light was appearing when he heard the river. He'd worked up a minor sweat that felt good, although it chilled him slightly. He stopped to take a leak, then slipped out of his pack, sat on a big rock, and drank a little coffee.

By the time Lucien reached the Rio Grande there was enough light to show him the far bank. He came to a clearing in the middle of which was a heavily used firesite. He and his father had caught trout and cooked them at this spot on many occasions. He pulled on his waders and boots, attached the reel to the rod, fed the line through the guides, connected a braided leader butt, and added a length of 5X tippet material. He stepped out into the current. He was rushing, he knew. He could hear his father telling him to study the river first, to note the possible lies in the pools and riffles, but he wanted to start. He roll cast upstream to some slower water. He almost always roll cast for some reason. The flow of the river was strong and as always a little troublesome at first, but soon he felt at home. It was easy to see then, and after a dozen or so casts, he spotted the rise of a trout just upstream from where he had been fishing earlier. He cast to the far side of where he had seen the fish and let the current bring the fly back to him. He cast again, saw the fly disappear, and gave the line a tug to set the hook. He could never get over the excitement of catching a fish, of tricking a fish. His heart fluttered and he played the trout in. It was a ten-inch rainbow, nothing to get crazy about, but it was a decent fish. He removed the fly from the animal's lip and let it go, first holding it facing the current until it felt strong.

He fished for a couple of hours, catching two more trout of about the same size, then stopped for a sandwich and coffee before working his way upstream to the confluence of the two rivers.

When Lucien got to the place where the rivers met, he was surprised to find another fisherman sitting on the bank. He looked at the man and realized that he knew him. The short, pudgy Indian was Warren Fragua, a deputy sheriff who had been a friend of his father's.

"Mr. Fragua?"

"Hello." The man tried to place Lucien.

"Lucien Bradley. Henry Bradley's son."

"Oh yeah. You're in the army." He shook Lucien's hand.

"Not anymore." Lucien hated having people define him by his army association. "I just got home."

Fragua nodded. "I'm sorry about your father."

"Yeah."

They looked at the river.

"He was a hell of a fisherman," Fragua said.

"Yes sir." Lucien stretched. "You been doing any good out here?"

"Doing okay. Nothing to write home about."

"I caught three ten-inchers downriver a ways."

Fragua yawned. "So you're home. I know your mother's happy about that. What are you going to do?"

"Don't know yet. Get a job, I guess. Go back to school maybe."

"You're young. You've plenty of time."

"Are you still with the sheriff's office?"

"Yep."

"Must be pretty interesting."

"Sort of. There's not much excitement around these parts, as you well know. I think that's why I keep doing it. It pays the bills and I can fish. What did you do in the army?"

Lucien smiled. "What does anybody do in the army? Waited to get out."

Fragua laughed softly, his eyes on the river.

"Well," Lucien said, "I'm going to work my way on up the Red here."

"Check you later, Lucien." Fragua called to Lucien when he was some yards away. "It's good to see you."

Lucien fished his way up the Red River. Most things didn't make any sense. He'd been home less than twenty-four hours and already he felt deeply unsettled and anxious and ready to call himself a bum or a vagrant or some kind of freeloader. He was afraid he was going to end up living his life one paycheck to the next like his friends from high school.

He didn't have any further luck with the trout that morning—even when he floated a Jassid beetle down a riffle, a method he usually considered cheating—but he didn't care.

He ate his last sandwich, washed it down with water from his canteen, and began the hike back up to his truck.

When Lucien walked into the house at noon he was nearly ready to fall over. Sleep kept nudging him and his mother offered a smile shy of laughter when she saw him. He sighed, walked past her and into his room where he managed to get out of most of his clothes before passing out. He was even sleepy in his dream.

In his dream, he was stumbling through a dense forest following the sound of a woman crying. Birds were screaming, monkeys were speaking from branches, water was dripping from giant leaves of a canopy that let in limited light. He worked to make himself alert, to keep his eyes open, to focus on something, anything, and there in front of him, open-mouthed and silent, nailed to a tree was the figure of Jesus, turning from flesh to wood to carbon. In the woods, he came upon a bed in which his father, missing many pounds and dressed in a hospital gown, lay dying. The dying man swung his legs around, landed his feet on the floor of matted leaves, stood up, and began to pace.

"So, you've finally come to see me," his father said, walking away toward a flowering tree. He turned and walked back.

"I'm sorry."

The man started for the tree again, then whipped around, clutching his gown. "Ha! Caught you! Didn't I? Admit it, I caught you peeking at your old man's crack. Damn these gowns." He staggered to the bed and sat.

"Dad, I'm sorry."

"Shut the hell up. Stop apologizing." He leaned back and put his head on the pillow. "Death is really fucked up, Lucien. It has its downside."

"What's that?"

"It's only temporary. Life goes on forever, but death is only temporary."

Lucien rubbed his eyes and watched shapes fade in and out. "I don't get it."

"What's your favorite color, son?"

"Dun."

Lucien watched his father close his eyes and begin to swell, first his face, his cheeks pressing beyond their limits, then his neck and arms. Christ was talking now, strange words that were not clear. Lucien looked at Jesus and said, "But I don't know you." And all was silent.

Throwing Earth

Joseph Martin straightened, cracking his back. He winced, and a sigh of release softened his face. Letting the pitchfork rest against the stall wall, he twisted his torso again but heard no sound. He leaned his head and shoulders past the gate and called out to his son.

Wes left the water trough he was watching fill up and walked across the hard-baked ground of the corral toward the barn.

"I want you to finish up in here," Joseph said, stepping out of the stall and stomping his boots to free the clinging dung and straw. He watched the boy set to work. "I'm going to take a look at your mother's car."

The boy paused, particles from a pitched load settling. "She ain't here."

Joseph pushed up his hat and raked at the perspiration on his forehead with the back of his hand. "She told me her car was acting up." He looked toward the house. "Where'd she go? She say?"

"I don't know, Daddy."

Joseph looked at the horizon, and the hot, dusty day. "When you finish in here, come get me and we'll worm the last of the horses."

The boy nodded and Joseph left him to work.

Joseph went to the house and stopped in the kitchen to pour himself a glass of cold water from the bottle in the refrigerator. He held the glass against his face, looking around for a note that his wife might have left. He thought about replacing the leaky T-pipe at the top of the water heater, but instead went outside and sat beneath the big cottonwood. He soaked up shade and watched the driveway, the road, the magpies, the jays.

Wes came to the front yard and stood by Joseph, stunned momentarily by the shade. "Ready to do the horses?"

Joseph stood up.

"What were you doing, Daddy?"

"Nothing."

"I got the medicine out."

"Good." Joseph slapped a hand on Wes's shoulder. "Good." They walked to the small corral beyond the barn.

"Daddy, you think it'd be all right if I went out for the basketball team this year?"

Joseph smiled. "Sure, why not?"

"Just figured I'd ask. I know there's a lot to do around here."

Joseph looked at his son and for the first time actually noticed his height. "When did you get as tall as me?"

"Taller," Wes said.

Joseph pressed his back against the tiled wall of the shower. Once, more of his body struck flush; now his shoulders curved over a bit. Dirt and dust followed rivulets down his body, twisting off his tired legs and finding the drain. He turned off the water and dried his body roughly with a white towel that was stiff from hanging on the line.

While he dressed he listened to his wife downstairs in the kitchen; he heard her footsteps, the clattering of plates and pots settling on the table. She was whistling. The tune annoyed Joseph, but he couldn't help listening closely. He laughed softly at himself, discovering his anger, but the emotion was no surprise. He was only startled by the calm of it all.

He dressed in new jeans and a white shirt and went downstairs. He sat at the dining-room table, where he always sat, his back to the window.

Wes said nothing, just tore into his meal, keeping his eyes cast down at his busy plate.

"How's your car?" Joseph asked.

Cora was not ready with an answer. Her voice broke as she searched for words. She landed on, "It did fine today, for a while, but the noise started again."

"The squeaking you described?" he asked, not really paying attention to her, but tossing a sidelong glance toward the boy.

"Yes," she said.

He nodded and mumbled that he would tend to it later. He asked Wes to pass the bread. After a silence he asked, "By the way, where'd you go earlier?"

Her response was ready and clear and its suddenness pulled Wes's eyes from his fork to her. "I was at Amy's house, helping her choose wallpaper for her kitchen."

"She doing it herself or having somebody come in?" Joseph buttered his roll.

"Having somebody come in," Cora said. "And of course I picked up some groceries."

The moon was unrelenting as Joseph stared out the bedroom window. The cornbread globe, just shy of full, sang a glow of restful light, but Joseph was up cursing it. He went to the window and looked down at the bay mare in the pasture. He couldn't climb back into bed. He couldn't lie between the sheets with that woman; he couldn't have her foot brush his leg or her hair tickle his shoulders. He pulled on his pants and went down the stairs, outside, and across the yard to the corral. The night was cool and not very dark. He took up a handful of earth and looked at it. He knew that if he threw it as hard and as far as he could, all of it would still fall on his land. He let the dirt sift through his fingers.

The next weeks saw a steady rain that had come late, but had come. The pastures were soft and the horses stayed near the trees in the corner of the pasture. Cora's car was gone more and more. He had seen her car parked in the same place in town several times. Refusing to acknowledge that a blind eye is just as vulnerable as one that sees, he went about his work, rising early, falling silent in the evenings. He could see her car in his sleep, through the windshield of his truck, the rain rolling down it, the wipers counting cadence.

Finally one day he greeted her with the same face he had for weeks and told her that he knew. She smiled, a cutting, wicked smile, Joseph thought, and his calm faded, his eyes narrowed and hardened. His brain spoke to her, telling her to feel his pain, the hurt of the betrayal, telling her to open his shirt and see the gaping wound.

Cora's smile went away and she was afraid.

Joseph did nothing, said nothing. "Wes," he called to his son.

Wes came into the room.

"Come on, let's ride into town."

Wes looked at his parents, one then the other. "Okay."

Joseph did not offer Cora another glance. He followed Wes out the door and through the drizzle to the truck. It was dusk as they stopped at a diner.

Wes waited until they were seated and had ordered before he asked, "What's going on?"

"Your mother and I are having some problems."

"No kidding."

Joseph looked at his son, not knowing what to say or whether he should say anything. "She's been cheating on me, Wes."

The boy looked at his father.

"She's been with another man."

Wes shook his head and looked out the window. "I don't believe you. Who?"

"Doesn't matter."

The waitress brought the food.

Wes looked at his chicken-fried steak and moved it with his fork. "So, what's going to happen?"

Joseph shrugged, and drank some coffee.

Joseph and Wes came home to a dark house. They said good night and Wes went upstairs to bed. Joseph sat in the kitchen for a few minutes, then climbed the stairs to the room he shared with Cora, and found her in bed. He sat on the edge of his side, holding his hands, his elbows resting on his knees. He heard her stir and sit up.

"Joseph, we have to talk about this," she said, her voice looking for steadiness.

He wanted something to happen, wanted to talk, but he didn't have the stomach for it. He stood up.

"Don't leave," she said.

He turned to face her and she switched on the bedside lamp.

"I'm not leaving, Cora," he said, "not this ranch anyway. And I'm not going to ask you to leave. But I'm not asking you to stay."

"I'm sorry," she said.

"Yeah, well, maybe this will blow over. I don't know." He turned and walked away from her, but stopped at the door. "I don't want to know who it was."

"It didn't, doesn't mean anything," she said.

Without looking at her, he said, "Oh, it means something." He rubbed a hand over his head.

She said, "I want you to talk to Wes."

"And tell him what?"

Cora switched off the lamp and lay back down. He could tell

her eyes were open, fixed on the ceiling. He could feel her not look-ing at him.

Joseph stepped away, leaned against the wall outside his room and looked at his son's bedroom door. Talk to him? He didn't know what to tell him. He didn't know what to tell himself.

It was hot again. Joseph was just about to climb the ladder and find out what was wrong with the vapor lamp on the barn. His stomach had felt uneasy all morning and now there was a pain in his gut. It had been giving him trouble for a couple weeks, but he had waved it off. He swayed a bit, thought about the dizziness, and passed out.

He awoke to the drawling voice of the retired doctor from Tennessee who lived down the road. The obtrusive space between his teeth made him hard to look at. Joseph sat up, and noticed he had been moved to his bed. His wife stood at the foot of the bed.

"Just a bug, eh, Doc?" Joseph said.

The doctor shrugged. "I can't say. You need to go in and 'get looked at,' as we say."

"Thank you, Dr. Wills," Cora said.

"Yeah, thanks, Doc," Joseph said, not looking at the man but out the window.

Once Cora led the doctor out of the room, Joseph wrapped an arm across his tender middle, and stood up despite the pain. He went to the window and looked out. Wes was on the ladder fixing the light. Wes looked back at the house and saw his father. The boy climbed down and came running across the yard to the house.

Wes came upstairs and gave Joseph a hug.

"Thanks for fixing the light."

"I knew you wanted it done." He studied his father. "Shouldn't you be lying down?"

"I'm okay," Joseph said.

Cora appeared, and stood in the doorway. Wes ignored her. Cora sighed and left.

"Don't treat your mother like that," Joseph said.

"Yes, sir."

Joseph rubbed the hair on his son's head roughly. "Since when am I a sir?"

"I don't know."

"Go see what you can do to help your mother while I lie down for a while."

Wes left the room.

Cora made an appointment for Joseph with the same doctor her father had gone to some months earlier. He drove into the city for the preliminary examination, which was short enough but ended with an invitation to return.

"Didn't they say anything?" Cora asked when he returned. "They must have said something."

"What do you care?"

Wes stepped into the kitchen just in time to hear his father's words.

"Just that I have to come back," Joseph said.

"Not even a hunch?"

He shrugged. "Said something about it maybe being an ulcer." He sat at the kitchen table to eat the cold meat sandwich she had made for him.

"That's what it is," she said. "You hold things in. And you don't eat right, Joseph."

He nodded and looked at his son. "I guess I do," he said, turning to look into his wife's eyes.

"That's what it is," she said.

Joseph went out to the pasture fence and looked at his horses. Wes followed him.

"How you feeling?" the boy asked.

"Fine. Ulcer."

The boy spat into the dust and covered it with the toe of his boot. "They give you pills?"

"Not yet." He put a foot up on the lowest rail of the fence. "Everything's fine, Wes." He coughed into a fist. "You any good at this basketball stuff?"

Wes chuckled. "I'm okay."

"I'm glad you're going to play," Joseph said. "It'll keep you out of trouble."

"Right. That's why I'm playing."

The next visit to the doctor started early, one test followed by another. The congenial grins faded into knitted brows. Then he was given an endoscopic examination that fascinated and scared him. A lighted tube was passed down his throat and into his stomach. Calipers were fed through the tube to extract tissue that was biopsied by pathologists who Joseph imagined deep in the basement of the University Hospital.

Joseph sat by the doctor's desk and watched the man light a cigarette and blow out a cloud of blue smoke. "How's the ranch, Joseph?"

"Fine."

"Good bunch of foals this year?"

"I've seen better."

The doctor put out his cigarette, looking at it with a bit of disgust. "Joseph, it seems we have a problem."

Joseph nodded.

"We have gastrointestinal lymphomas."

"We do?"

The doctor cleared his throat. "Infiltrates have embedded themselves into your stomach wall. That's why we thought ulcer at first." He coughed. "It's serious. We're in trouble."

"How much trouble?" Joseph asked.

"Chemotherapy might help, but I can't make any promises."

"Are you telling me we're dying?"

"Yes, I am," the doctor said. "You want it straight, Joseph?"

"Of course."

"I wish I could say something good. My guess, well it's more than a guess, is that treatment will only keep you alive a little longer. But who knows? The body is an amazing thing." He studied Joseph's face. "I'd like you to come back next week and we'll run the tests again." He pulled a small white pad of paper in front of him and started to write. He glanced up at Joseph. "Here's something for the pain."

Joseph took the prescription and stuffed it into his shirt pocket. He stood up and shook the doctor's hand.

"You all right?" the doctor asked.

Joseph smiled. "Apparently not."

Joseph thought about his wife as he drove his pickup out of the parking lot of the medical center. Cora was no pessimist. He knew that she believed with every ounce of herself that her husband would step through the front door and tell her that he was all right. He knew she expected this and so he planned to lie. Just an ulcer, he would say, then stand witness to her relief. And she would tell him again that it was because he held things in. At a stoplight in the middle of town he recalled how much he disliked the city; he couldn't see any purpose in living like that. He also failed to see the point in telling a lie like the one he had planned, a lie that could not be maintained indefinitely. He would tell Cora the truth and be with her while she came to terms with things. He would tell her, she would stiffen a little, straighten her back, and say that they would see their way through. Then he'd tell her that he was refusing treatment because it would only moderately prolong his life and greatly enhance his suffering, at which point she would fall to the floor crying and cursing him. Truth of the matter was he had no idea how it would go, or even if he would have the courage to tell her.

Joseph was thirty-eight, a young man. He was younger with the passing of every block as he left the city behind. He saw some teenagers on the basketball courts of a middle school. He parked and went to stand by the far goal, where he leaned against the post. An errant pass bounced his way. He stopped the ball and picked it up, held it.

"Mind if I take a shot?" he asked.

They told him to go ahead. He put his hat on the ground and stepped forward, dribbled a couple of times. He threw up a thirty-foot jumper that bounced long off the rim back to him. He walked closer to the basket, bouncing the ball slowly, feeling it rise each time to meet his palm and fingers.

"Come on, man, shoot," said one of the boys.

"Why don't you try guarding me?" Joseph said. A breeze pushed at his back.

The boys laughed and the one who had told him to hurry came forward, flashing a smile back at his buddies. He was a tall boy with long arms and fancy basketball shoes. He took a quick swipe at the ball, but Joseph turned his body.

"Make a move, old man."

Joseph gave the kid a head fake and dribbled left. The kid stayed with him, so he spun right on the heel of his boot and put a fall-away jumper.

"Yes," Joseph said as the ball banged around the rim and fell through the hole. "How do you like it, sonny?"

The boys teased their friend. The kid shrugged it off, got the ball, and dribbled to the top of the key. He pointed at Joseph and gestured for him to come. Joseph smiled and went to him. The kid tried to drive right, but Joseph stepped over and stopped him. Joseph feigned a move for the ball and the boy almost lost control of it.

"Okay, old man," the teenager said and made a quick move again to the right.

Joseph was caught flat-footed in his heavy cowboy boots and fell a full step behind. Joseph reached out and pushed the kid in the back. The shot went wild and the boy fell and rolled across the blacktop into the grass.

The kid got up. "What's the matter with you, man?" The other boys rallied behind him.

Joseph was confused, but angry and he found himself stepping up to the kid. "What's the problem?" He squinted up at the sun. "Are you mad at me?" he asked the boy. The kid looked at him like he was crazy; he was ready to back away, ready to run, but Joseph wouldn't let him. "You're mad at me. I can see that. You want to hit me, don't you? Don't you?"

"Nah, man, I don't want to hit you. I just want you to go away."

"Come on," Joseph said. He knew what it felt like to be a jerk. He pushed his chin out. "Punch for punch, midface. You go first."

"You're crazy," the kid said.

Joseph moved closer. He was just inches from the boy's face, and could see him sweating. "Don't be scared."

"I'm not scared."

"Why don't you just go someplace?" another boy said.

Joseph silenced the smaller boy with a look and returned his attention to the first kid. Joseph pushed the boy in the chest with both hands. "I said for you to hit me."

The boy fell back a step and swallowed hard, his eyes wide open. "Hey, man."

Joseph shoved him again.

The other teenagers stepped in and stood between them. They

were all unsteady, heaving in deep breaths, shifting their weight left to right.

"Go home," the kid said from behind his friends.

"All right, I'll go home, but first I want you to punch me. Hey, I've been an asshole out here. A real asshole. I won't hit you back, I promise. You can't let somebody be such a jerk and get away with it."

"Go on and hit him, John," one of the boys said.

"Yeah," said another.

"I don't want to," John said.

"Your pals are here, so I can't very well hit you back, right?" Joseph felt a smile on his face, an unfamiliar smile, a hollow smile, a mean smile.

The kid squeezed through his friends and Joseph thrust out his chin again and pointed to it. The boy threw out a weak open-handed tap that Joseph barely felt on his cheek.

"Harder," Joseph said, pointing again to his chin. "Right there."

Another blow, a little sharper. The boy was trembling, his lips parted and quivering.

"Hit me like a man!"

"Let him have it, John."

"Yeah."

When Joseph came around, he was alone. The sun was almost gone and a light drizzle was falling. His face hurt. The wind blew trash across the blacktop. His brain throbbed. A violent shudder ran through his body as he thought about what he had done. He wanted to find the boy he had terrorized and apologize. Then he hoped that the punch had been good enough, satisfying for him, hoped that the boy's fear would be short-lived, hoped he would never see him again. Maybe all the boys would get a good laugh out of it. They would be nervous and falsely cocky at first, Joseph imagined, but later genuine laughter. "John, remember that crazy . . ." he could hear them saying.

He felt better when he could see the hills scissor-cut against the western sky. It was dark when he rolled home. The night smelled good. When he entered the house he found there was little need to tell Cora anything. She looked at his swollen face and started to cry. She begged him not to die.

"Okay," he said. He held her for a while there by the door and took deep breaths, thought about things like insurance and debts.

She pulled from him and walked stiffly away.

Joseph went into the bathroom and looked at his face in the mirror, rubbed his jaw.

Wes came in.

"Hey there, cowboy," Joseph said. He could hear Cora crying in the bedroom.

"You okay?"

"Nah, I guess I'm not doing so hot."

"What happened to your jaw?" the boy asked.

"Tried to knock some sense into myself." He looked at Wes's face in the mirror. "Why don't you see about your mother?"

Squeeze

"You sure you ain't got no Indian blood in you?" the heavily mustached Lucius Carter asked again.

Jack Winston castrated the bull and tossed the severed parts behind him where they landed in the dirt at the base of the shed wall.

Carter rubbed the neck of his bay, which chomped its bit and stamped the parched ground. He looked down at the man kneeling behind the young bull confined in the squeeze gate. "Just a touch?"

"Carter, if you weren't studyin' your ropes all the damn time, you'd see I'm black and nothing else." He smiled at the man working the squeeze. Several men within earshot laughed while they worked, since Winston had insulted Carter's ability as a cowboy.

Carter pushed his tongue into his cheek and stared hard at Winston for a second before spitting and walking away. He pushed the shoulder of another hand who said something to him as he passed.

"You got him a good one that time," Kirby Dodds said and let the bull go.

Winston didn't want to get him "a good one." Winston didn't want to say anything. He gave injections to and castrated three more bulls, watched them bolt away from the gate, then stood up, slapped at his dusty knees, and headed for the bunkhouse. He shed his smelly shirt, sat down on the foot of his bed, closed his eyes, and took a deep, dusty breath. He raised an arm and worked a kink out of his shoulder, then pulled off his boots and socks and wiggled his toes.

Jubal Dixon, the cook, a short, one-legged man, appeared at the doorway, looked past Winston out the window, then asked, "You eating here?"

"No, Jubal, I thought I'd drive into Deer Point, get a room and wash my filthy, stinking clothes. Maybe catch a ball game on television."

Jubal nodded and turned away.

"Hey, Jubal," Winston called after him. "Want to ride in with me?"

Jubal considered the offer as he leaned against the jamb and tapped the floor with his metal crutch.

"What do you say?"

"Split a room?"

"You bet."

Winston showered and gathered together his dirty clothes in a couple of pillowcases. He put on his good boots and good hat and stood by his truck waiting for Jubal. Jubal came out with a small knapsack, wearing a brand new pair of jeans; the empty leg was neatly folded up and pinned behind him. He tugged at the lapels of his corduroy sports coat.

"Jubal, you've got to give the gals a fightin' chance."

"Ready?"

Winston watched as Jubal climbed in on the passenger side, then got in himself and started the engine. He pulled the Jeep pickup around past the corral, onto the wagon-rutted lane, and followed that to the gravel road.

"How do you like this thing?" Jubal asked.

"Can't complain. I've gotten six years out of her."

"I been thinking about getting me one of them Rangers. You like those?"

"Good trucks," Winston said. "I wouldn't turn one down."

"Wouldn't kick it out of bed, huh?" Jubal said and laughed. "Wouldn't kick it out of bed," he repeated more softly, shaking his head and grinning.

Winston smiled at the joke.

It was dusk and Jubal was just coming to from a nap with a jerking of his leg and coughing in a closed mouth. Winston had enjoyed the talkless time by just looking out at the countryside. Jubal cleared his throat and rustled around until Winston glanced over at him. The younger man wasn't sure what he was seeing at first. He did a double take, leaning over to see more clearly. Jubal had a rag in his hand and was rubbing it against something in his lap. It was his teeth. He had his dentures out of his face and in his lap and was polishing them with his hankerchief. Winston didn't say anything, just kept his eyes forward on the road.

There wasn't much to the town of Deer Point, but folks claimed it was a town. There was a hotel, a couple of bars, a Dairy Queen, a Sears catalog store, a traffic light that was turned off on the weekends, and a Chinese restaurant name Lung Luck's. They registered at the New Deer Point Hotel, which had been built in 1892 and was called "New" even though no "Old" Deer Point Hotel had ever existed. Winston began up the wide stairway slowly, anticipating Jubal's pace, but Jubal vaulted up the carpeted steps to the second-floor landing with his crutch swinging close to his leg.

"Easier to do it fast," Jubal said, turning to face Winston at the top.

They dropped off their gear, left the hotel, and went down the street to Lung Luck's. They sat at a table in the middle of the restaurant, placed their orders, and soon their food was brought to them. The kitchen radio was playing country music that became louder every time the waiter passed through the swinging door.

"Know what I heard a feller call this stuff once?" Jubal said, pointing at his food with his fork. "Chink Stink."

Winston glanced at the waiter to see if he had heard. It seemed he hadn't since he continued to wipe down a booth table without pause.

"Always liked it myself," Jubal said. "Didn't much care for that feller."

Winston nodded and bit into an egg roll.

"That same guy would let his dog lick his dishes clean. I mean, that's how he washed 'em."

They ate on for a couple of minutes in silence. Jubal's crutch, which was leaning against an empty chair, began to slide to the floor. The man caught it.

"I ever tell you how I lost my leg?"

Winston shook his head. "No occasion to hear that story, I'm afraid."

"I was out lookin' for cows on BLM land. I saw a steer and took off after it. I didn't see the ravine and neither did the damn horse and we both flipped in the air and the son of a bitch landed on me." He drank some iced tea. "Feller that was ridin' with me went for help and forgot where in blazes I was. Can you believe some shit like that? Then, by the time they found me . . ." He paused. "Infection."

"Hm," Winston said.

"And you know who that feller was?" Jubal didn't wait for a reply. "It was the idiot with the dish-licking pooch. Dog spit probably got into his brain and made him loco."

They paid up and went down the street to a tavern called the Stirrup that held a big lighted sign with a tilted martini glass — the olive was rolling back and forth. Winston and Jubal drank beers and ate nuts and played pool. Jubal shot pool with his crutch and he was doing pretty good until the beers started to take hold; his balance became uncertain, his shooting got sloppy, and the rubber tip of his crutch threatened to scratch the cloth. They walked over to a booth and sat down. Jubal drummed his fingers on the Formica—his nails were in need of trimming—and drank beer from a bottle.

"I think that ought to be your last one," Winston said.

Jubal didn't seem to hear him and looked away at the door. "Jesus Christ," he moaned, "Lookie what the cat drug in."

Winston looked up to see Lucius Carter, in a new white hat, with another man and a broad-shouldered, heavily made-up woman. Her eye shadow was evident even from across the room and it extended well beyond her brows.

Lucius saw Winston and the one-legged man and made straight for their booth. "How you boys?" he asked.

Winston and Jubal nodded. Winston knew Jubal didn't much like Carter.

"Couldn't find no ladies, so you had to settle for each other, eh?" Carter said.

Jubal looked at the blond woman who had come in with the other man. "See you couldn't find no ladies either."

Carter smiled an evil smile. "What was that?"

"You heard me," Jubal said, looking him in the eye.

Winston sighed.

"How do you think you'd get around with no legs, Hoppy?" Carter said.

Winston grabbed Jubal's arm as he started to rise. "Steady, cowboy."

"Yeah," Carter said, "better keep your girlfriend under control."

Jubal snatched free of Winston's grasp, stood, and swung his crutch, which caused Lucius Carter to duck and step back. "Son of a bitch," he shouted. Winston found himself standing, too. Jubal swayed there for a moment while the alcohol found his brain and then he passed out.

The blond and the second man came and stood with Carter over the unconscious man. Winston gathered him up, loaded him over his shoulder, grabbed his crutch, and walked out. He carried the man down the street and through the lobby of the New Deer Point Hotel, past a clump of tourists who probably thought this was a neat piece of local color, or maybe they thought the dusty black cowboy was taking the one-legged, unconscious, old man upstairs to have his way with him. He climbed the stairs and wedged Jubal between his shoulder and the wall while he got the door open. He dropped him onto one of the beds.

He sat at the window and looked out at the quiet street. It was a lonely life, he thought. Then he heard gurgling, coughing, and he saw that Jubal was having some kind of problem. He leaned over him. Jubal was choking because his dentures had gotten turned sideways in his mouth.

Winston sighed long. A cowboy touched a lot of things, he thought, blood, dung, placenta, but here he was, stone-chilled by the prospect of reaching in and pulling out the man's dentures. But he did it. With a deep, held breath, he did it. He dropped the teeth on the nightstand between the beds and ran into the bathroom and washed his hands for a considerable time, nearly disappearing one of those little wafers of hotel soap.

He thought about turning on the television, but instead just undressed, opened the window wider, got into bed, and closed his eyes.

Next morning, Winston woke up and showered while Jubal was still unconscious, his snoring letting on that he was alive. Winston didn't disturb him, just grabbed his sack of laundry and left the room.

While his clothes were in the machine he read back issues of *Sports Illustrated* and *Newsweek* and *McCall's* and smiled at a little Indian girl who kept running down the aisle away from her mother, rolling a plastic bottle of fabric softener.

"How are you?" Winston asked the girl as he folded a pair of jeans.

The four-year-old just stared at him. She had big dark eyes and straight black hair that fell down her back in two braids. She was wearing a sweatshirt with a bear on it.

"My name is Jack. What's yours?" He smiled at the woman who didn't seem to mind him talking to the child.

"Mary Dreamer."

"That's a pretty name."

The girl ran back to her mother, pausing to pick up a fabric-softener sheet off the floor. Her mother snatched it from her and threw it into the trash.

A man in a dirty coat with greasy, matted hair came in and pushed through the magazines on the counter before asking the woman for change. The woman pulled her daughter behind her and told him to go away. He walked over to Winston, smiled big, and showed a mouth with two lonely teeth. Winston could smell the whisky and, before the man could ask, gave him two quarters.

"Thanks, pard," the man said in a loud voice, flashed the smile again, and went away.

The woman frowned at Winston, he assumed because he had given the scary man some money. Still, he said good-bye to the girl as he left.

When he got back to the room he saw that it had been ransacked. The sheets were off the bed and lying on the floor. One side of the drapes had been yanked down. Jubal was hopping around on his leg and pulling at his hair.

"What's happening here?" Winston asked, dropping his laundry inside the door. He glanced quickly, nervously behind him and shut the door. "What are you doing?"

"My grinners. I can't find my grinners." Jubal looked at Winston with a pathetic face.

"You were choking on them last night, Jubal, so I took them out."

Jubal looked sick. Here was a man who once sucked milk from a cow's teat on a dare, but the idea of a man reaching into his mouth was about to make him ill.

"You were choking," Winston said.

Jubal hopped back and sat on his bed.

"I put them on the nightstand." Winston pointed and started toward the table.

"Well, they ain't there now," Jubal said and he shot up. "Jesus H. Christ on TV, somebody done stole my grinners."

Winston was confused, dizzy, and he didn't know what he was saying, but words came out. "I'll go look outside." With that he hurried out. He stood in the hallway looking at the closed door. There was no reason for him to go outside in search of the dentures, but he went anyway. It was someplace other than in that room.

He went out, leaned against the outside wall of the building, looked up at the sky, and let the sun hit his face. He blew out a breath, then found himself looking at the sidewalk and gutter and street. He heard humming coming from down the block and he glanced over to spot the lean man from the Laundromat walking his way. He looked back into the gutter.

"Howthodo," the man said.

Winston studied the man and frowned.

"Howthodo."

Winston leaned in close. "Say something else."

"Wha thu wa ma sa?" The drunk's mouth seemed peculiar. He had teeth, more that just the lonely two he'd shown before, weird teeth that seemed to move around.

Winston pointed at his mouth. "Where'd you get those?" he asked.

The man spat the dentures out into his dirt-crusted hand. "I bought 'em."

Winston looked up at the window of his room. "How much did you pay for them?"

"A buck."

"I'll give you five for them," Winston said.

The man pondered, then said, "Hell, they don't fit no way." He took the five-dollar bill from Winston and placed the teeth in his open palm.

Winston nearly fainted, actually swayed before collecting himself enough to sprint across the hotel lobby, and into the public rest room. He set the teeth on the sink and began to wash his hands furiously. One of the tourists standing at a neighboring sink seemed frightened. "Found my friend's teeth," Winston said. The man ran out. Winston washed for many minutes. He grabbed the dentures in a couple of paper towels and took them upstairs to the room.

"Found them," he said as he stepped in.

Jubal let out a sigh. "Thank you, Jesus, thank you, thank you," he said. He took them from Winston and paused. "Where'd you find them?"

Winston coughed, cleared his throat. "I found them in the street, Jubal, just lying there."

Jubal blew out a whistle between bare gums. "Good." He took them to the bathroom and held them under the water. He loaded them into his face and worked his jaw a bit.

Winston went to the window and started to put the room back together. He slipped the curtain hooks through the rod eyes. Below he could see the derelict turn the corner and pass out of sight.

"Just lying in the street, huh?" Jubal asked.

"Just lying there."

"Funny. Wonder how they got down there."

Winston turned to look at Jubal, thinking that the man didn't believe him. But Jubal showed nothing but puzzlement as he began to help put the room back together. Winston was pretty sure that Lucius Carter had come into the room and taken the teeth, but he wasn't going to talk about it with Jubal.

"You know, a man can walk in his sleep," Jubal said. "Won't have a notion in the morning of where he's been."

"Not uncommon," Winston said.

"I ain't never known myself to walk in my sleep."

"Hmmm," Winston said.

Jubal had the sheets and covers on top of the two beds and he sat down on his. "I want to thank you for helping me out last night. When I was choking, I mean."

"You bet."

"A dentist suggested I use some of that sticky stuff, you know, to hold my teeth firm, but I can't stand it. Too much maintenance."

Winston nodded, putting up the second curtain.

Jubal went to the window and looked at the street. "Just lyin' there," he said more to himself than to Winston. "Top and bottom together?"

"Mere inches apart."

"Flat out luck."

Winston worked a kink out of his shoulder. "Could be that I

got them stuck to my sack or sleeve or something when I went to do my laundry and they fell off outside."

The presence of even a lame explanation seemed to relax Jubal. He worked his bite. "Sun must have warped them a little."

"Sorry."

The older man waved it off. "Just glad to have 'em back. They'll mold back. Besides, if I'd choked to death . . ." He stopped. "What do you say we grab some chow and shoot some pool?"

"Okay."

It was ten o'clock in the morning, but late enough for burgers. Winston had a mug of milk with his food and talked a frowning Jubal into the same. They ate and shot a game and watched a boring baseball game on the set behind the bar. Every bite seemed an exercise for Jubal and Winston began to worry that the bum had damaged the dentures. He wondered if he needed to say something.

"Hey there, girls," Lucius Carter called to them.

Jubal had made up his mind to ignore the man. He went off to the rest room.

Lucius came to the table with a big ugly smile on his face.

Winston looked at him. "Funny stunt with a man's teeth."

Lucius laughed and looked at the two half-eaten burgers. "No harm done. He found 'em, didn't he?"

"Found them?" Winston felt hollow and a bit sick. "I wasn't there when he found them. Where were they?"

Lucius looked at Winston with a crooked smile. "Don't recall now."

"That sort of shit make you feel like a big man?" Winston was on the prod.

"Like I said, no harm done."

Winston slammed his cue stick down on the table. "Get the hell outta here!" His hand buzzed, he wanted to raise the stick high, but instead he let go.

The bartender called over, "No trouble."

"Out, Carter."

Lucius raised his hands. "Fine." He looked over at the bartender. "No trouble." He turned to Winston, smiled again and said, "Life's hard, but then the pay is low."

When Jubal came back out, Lucius was gone. "Where's the dung bank?"

"He left."

Jubal sat down behind his burger and rubbed his temples.

"How do your teeth feel?"

"Feel okay." Jubal looked at Winston. "What is it?"

"Nothing."

"How come you ain't eatin'?" Jubal asked.

"I'm not too hungry."

They left the tavern and got into Winston's truck. The sun was just past straight up and beating down on the cab. Winston looked before pulling out into the traffic.

"What do you think makes a fella end up like Lucius?" Winston asked.

"You mean, what makes him act the way he does?"

"Yeah." Winston switched on the radio.

"Too much sun," Jubal said. "Hell, I don't know. He must have been drowned at birth."

"Yeah, well."

"He sure hates you," Jubal said.

"Yep."

Jubal was looking at Winston. "He hates you 'cause you're colored."

"Black."

"Whatever. But that's why he hates you. Don't make no sense to me. You can't help what you are."

Winston looked at the man. "I don't need to help it."

"Whatever."

"How do you feel about the fact that I'm black?" Winston felt stupid asking the question.

"Don't make me no never mind. You could be purple for all I fuckin' care. Why all the questions?"

"I don't know."

They didn't say much during the rest of the drive. Winston watched the road and Jubal gazed out the window at the landscape. As they rolled to a stop near the bunkhouse, Winston said, "You know I don't mind that you're white, Jubal."

"Glad to hear it." Jubal paused before opening his door. "What made you think to say that?"

"Just lookin' at you," Winston said.

Big Picture

Michael walked out and down toward Massachusetts Avenue, hearing the horns of the traffic, smelling the exhaust, remembering how once he was passed up four times in the rain in D.C. by cabbies who wouldn't stop for a black man. The clincher was that two of the drivers had been black as well. It was a Thursday, the night of Washington's so-called "gallery walk"—"so-called" because, although some of the galleries in Adams-Morgan and Georgetown were within walking distance from one another, most were scattered all over the place, near Dupont Circle, well up Connecticut and downtown. Michael didn't really want to be there; he wasn't sure why he maintained a relationship with the small gallery. Washington was not terribly important in the art world, but the owner had been an early supporter of his. The owner was a flamboyantly gay man who had sold the occasional painting when Michael was starving and really needed a sale. Now, sales were common, and welcome, but the news of them did little to move Michael beyond the sense of loss he felt knowing the paintings were gone. Joshua, the gallery owner, had talked Michael into the show, telling him that Santa Fe, Los Angeles, and New York were not the only places where art happened.

"Where do you live, my lovely Michael?" Joshua had asked over the phone. "Do you live in Los Angeles, my sweet? No, you don't. Have you become so jaded and mainstream and, how shall I put it, American?"

It was the last word that had gotten under Michael's skin. Now the wonderful irony was that to prove to himself that he hadn't succumbed to some simple American idiocy about the location of art, he was having a show he didn't need in the nation's capital.

"Michael, oh, Michael," Joshua called, leaning out of the doorway of the gallery.

Michael turned and looked at him.

Joshua waved frantically for him to come back. "I need you!" he called.

Michael walked slowly back to him, wondering where Karen was. He last saw her talking and laughing with a woman from the *Post*. She liked these things more than he did.

When Michael was close, Joshua said softly, excitedly, "I think I've sold the big one."

A pain shot through Michael's head like a ricocheting bullet as he considered the six-by-eight-foot canvas that he had thought about withholding from the show. He had included it because of the strength of the work, believing that no one would buy it. "People aren't buying big anymore," Joshua had complained, hearing about the piece. It was also priced at a whopping thirty thousand dollars, more than twice as much as any of his other canvases in Santa Fe, Los Angeles, or New York.

"The big one?" Michael said.

"Can you believe it?" Joshua pulled him by the arm into the gallery, squeezing his bicep happily, lovingly. He led Michael to the canvas, in front of which stood about fifteen people.

Karen came over, kissed Michael's cheek, and wrapped herself about his other arm. Michael looked at her illuminated face, and found her way too happy. Karen had been his wife for less than a year; she was so young, innocent, as unblemished as her skin. He knew it was not the money that was exciting her, rather the electricity of everything, the people buzzing like shiny-eyed bees. She was guiltless, after all, but still it was disconcerting, agitating even, to see her as animated as she was, staring at the man in the double-breasted suit who stood so conspicuously before everyone, admiring the painting.

Michael took an instant dislike to the man, seeing his high-flown clothes as symptom, his exaggeratedly relaxed posture as contrivance.

"Douglass Dheaper," the double-breasted man said, reaching to shake Michael's hand. Upon taking it, he gave it a gentle, but imperious squeeze. "You are a genius," he said, turning back to admire the painting. "It's so daring, so reckless, impertinent even. Wouldn't you say so, Laura?" he said to the woman beside him who nodded her painted face. "Laura agrees."

"It's thirty thousand dollars," Michael said flatly.

"A steal," Dheaper said. "It's worth twice that." He smiled broadly, "But you've already stated a price, so there's no changing it." He laughed.

The people standing around laughed with him. Karen laughed too, but a look from Michael silenced her, causing him to feel immediately like a bully.

"It's not for sale," Michael said.

Laughter caught in their throats as they gasped.

Douglass Dheaper grinned smartly. "I beg your pardon?"

Joshua stepped in. "No, I beg your pardon," he said to Michael, pinching him on the arm.

Michael pulled away. "I don't like this guy. He's a phony and I don't want my painting near him."

Joshua pushed Michael into the office, closing the door, leaving behind Karen and the excitedly muttering mob. "Are you crazy?" he asked.

"Possibly. Definitely, if I let Mister Grease out there walk away with that painting." Michael rubbed his arm where Joshua had pinched him.

Joshua pointed to the sore spot. "And there's more where that came from." He paused to catch his breath. "That man, grease or no grease, was about to spend thirty thousand dollars. That would have been fifteen thousand dollars for you."

"It doesn't matter."

"What have you been doing? Is it the paint fumes?"

"I don't like him," Michael said.

"You don't have to like him."

"I don't want to sell the painting."

"That's too bad. We have an agreement."

Michael didn't say anything, but walked across the room and looked at a Klee print.

There was a knock at the door and when Joshua opened it, there was Dheaper, still smiling, really more of a smirk, looking past the older man for Michael.

"Is he okay?" Dheaper asked.

"Oh, he's fine," Joshua said. "You know how artists can be."

"Oh, I know," Dheaper said. "And I'm still going to buy the painting. I have to now."

Michael was staring at the man, confused.

Dheaper chuckled softly. "After that scene, the painting is going to be worth a bundle."

Joshua nodded, sharing the chuckle.

"And that reporter broad from the *Post* is out there, too. This is terrific." Dheaper looked right at Michael. "Good show, chum." With that, he backed out of the room and began to close the door, saying to Joshua, "This is really outstanding."

Michael fell into the chair behind the desk. "This is a dream. A nightmare."

"So, it worked out," Joshua said. "But that doesn't change the facts. You're nuts and childish and apparently don't care about anyone but yourself."

"Go fuck yourself," Michael said and rested his head on his arms on the desk. "Or whatever you people do."

"Oh, it's that way, is it?" Joshua said.

"No, it's not *that way*," Michael said. "I don't care what you do. All I know is, I don't want to fuck you. And I don't want you fucking me, which is what you just did out there."

Joshua stormed out and was replaced by Karen. "Are you all right?" she asked.

"No," he said without lifting his head.

"Oh, my sweet sensitive Michael," she said, coming around the desk to him and stroking his head. The way she was talking, he expected to hear her say, *Did the big bad man steal your wittle painting?* but instead she said, "I understand. There's so much of you in that canvas. It must be so hard."

"Come on, let's get out of here," he said, standing. "Let's go back to the hotel and go to bed."

During the cab ride back to the hotel, Michael was staring absently out the window and Karen was still whirring, petting his arm with measured touches, but he could feel her exhilaration.

"You liked all of that, didn't you?" he asked, turning to look at her in the dark.

"No," she said.

"You're still buzzing from it. I didn't like it. I'm dying inside. Do you understand what I'm telling you?"

Karen said nothing.

"Listen," he said, "I spent a lot of time on that canvas. I thought I could get that guy up on the price."

"You didn't think that," she said.

"Yes, I did. Didn't you hear him say it was worth twice that?"

"I don't believe you," she said.

"Don't believe me, then. It doesn't matter." Michael looked out the window again. "That's the last time I let that fucking Joshua handle a piece."

"It's his job to sell," Karen said. "He's not an artist."

"Neither am I," Michael snapped. "I'm a fraud, a phony, a pretender. I don't ever know what the hell I'm doing when I put paint on canvas."

Karen began to stroke his arm again.

Michael sighed.

In the hotel room, Karen sat at the desk and began to make a journal entry while Michael stripped to his boxers and watched television.

"Do you know why people never put televisions in paintings?" he asked. He didn't wait for her to say anything. "It's because no matter how you look at it, it looks stupid. Look at it now."

Karen did.

Michael tilted his head and flipped through a couple of stations with the remote. "Stupid, stupider, stupidest." He muted the sound and watched the mouths work harmlessly. "I can't paint anything that abstract."

Karen continued writing and Michael stayed with the soundless picture, but he was seething inside, aching; the thought of that man sitting in his greasy, gaudy, probably tidy home with that beautiful painting was killing him. Yes, it was beautiful perhaps, not because of its appearance, its colors, or its texture, but because of what was between the oils and the canvas: the sweat, the insecurities, the bad dreams, and the headaches. There was one spot in the picture, a spot smaller than a postcard, that Michael loved. Although put on wet together, Naples Yellow and Permanent Blue had not fused into green. The two colors remained so painfully separate that Michael wanted to cry each time he saw it.

Michael sat up.

"What is it?" Karen asked. "Is your head okay?"

"It's fine."

"I hate it when you lie about the pain," she said.

"Where's the phone book?"

"I don't know. In one of the drawers, I guess." She opened the drawer at the desk where she was sitting. "It's not in this one."

Michael opened and closed the drawers in the nightstands on both sides of the bed. Then he went to the closet and found it near the extra blanket. "Why would they stick the directory up here?"

"I don't know," Karen said. "Why do you need it?"

Michael didn't answer her, but sat on the bed beside the phone and started through the pages. He dialed and waited, looking over to find Karen silently, but aggressively waiting for a response to her last question.

"Hello," he said into the receiver. "Do you rent vans? You do. Do you have any? You do. What time do you close? Okay. This will be a one-way rental. To Denver, Colorado." Michael looked at Karen. "I'm on hold," he said.

"What are you doing?" she asked, coming around the desk to sit on the bed next to him, and looking at the yellow pages as if there were some clue to his thinking and actions there. "Michael?"

He paused her with a raised hand and then into the phone said, "Yes? How much? How much? Twenty-three hundred dollars? Are you sure?"

"Twenty-three hundred?" Karen echoed.

"I don't care," Michael said. "Can I come pick it up right away? A driver's license and a major credit card. No problem. What? I don't want to get it in the morning. No, I'm coming to pick it up now. I don't care about that. See you in a few minutes." Michael hung up.

"What in the world?" Karen said.

"Get packed," Michael said. "We're checking out."

"Checking out? Wait a second. Let's slow down here. I don't understand what's going on."

Michael stopped taking his socks and underwear out of a drawer of the dresser and said, "We're going to take that painting home with us."

"You can't do that."

"It's my painting."

"It's sold."

"I'm unselling it."

Karen shook her head, almost smiling. "Would you please just sit down and take a minute to think about this?"

"No. Just get packed. Please get packed. Actually, it doesn't matter whether you get packed now. You've got a plane ticket. I'll meet you in Denver."

"Do you honestly think Joshua is just going to hand over that painting to you?" she asked.

"Do you honestly think I'm going to ask for that bastard's permission?"

"Then how are you going to get in?"

"I'll meet you in Denver."

"You're not going to break in, are you?"

Michael stopped packing and sat down in a chair. "I have to do this. I know it sounds crazy, but I've got to do it. Now, I've got," he looked at the clock, "forty-three minutes to get over to the car-rental place. I'll understand if you fly home. In fact, that's a better plan. Okay?"

"I'm coming with you."

"Whatever. I don't have time to discuss it either way." He resumed packing.

"I'm coming with you," Karen repeated and started packing her clothes along with him.

The car rental was part of a chain, and was located on New York Avenue not far from the hotel. The place was surrounded by a twelve-foot, chain-link fence with razor wire spiraled along its top, and fat circles of white light spilled from evenly spaced floods on the sides of the building. The cars and trucks huddled in clumps as if for protection, and Michael, even in his raving state, managed a pun silently, thinking the cars were waiting to be jumped. The Ethiopian taxi driver waited while Michael and Karen spoke to the intercom at the gate. Michael looked into the closed-circuit camera and spoke loudly.

"I'm here to pick up a van," he said.

"What's your reference number?" a static-covered, lethargic voice asked.

"You didn't give me a reference number."

"We give everybody a reference number."

"Let's just go," Karen said.

"My name is Lawson. Don't you remember talking to me? The van to Denver?"

"I remember, but I need the reference number," the voice insisted.

"You didn't give me one, you asshole."

There was silence from the speaker.

"I'm here to rent a van for twenty-three-fucking-hundred dollars. I want to know what your fucking name is so I can tell your fucking boss why I had to go to fucking Avis to rent a fucking van."

The gate made a loud double-clack as it unlocked and Michael pushed it ajar, then waved the taxi driver on. He and Karen carried their bags across the asphalt lot, past the clusters of cars and vans to the door where they were briefly scrutinized by yet another camera before being let in. The attendant was seated behind a metal table, his pajama bottoms and bedroom slippers visible for all the world to see. Michael looked at the man, frowning. His age was a mystery—the ratty blond beard, crew cut, and the red eyes set into sallow sockets. Michael felt sick.

"I was sure I gave you a reference number," the man said.

Michael didn't say anything, but opened his wallet to find his license and credit card.

"This is a rough neighborhood," the man said. "You can't be too careful. They would just as soon eat your liver as look at you."

"Who's they?" Michael asked.

"Them punks."

Michael put the cards on the table.

"All the way to Denver, eh?"

Karen nodded, looking around.

"Don't worry ma'am," the attendant said. "This place is sealed up tighter than a flea's asshole."

"How nice," Karen said.

"But once you leave this yard, well, may God have mercy on you."

"Shut up," Michael said. "Charge it to the card and I don't want the insurance."

"Yes, sir."

"Michael, let's forget this and take a cab back to the hotel," Karen said, pulling at the sleeve of his jacket, pleading with her eyes.

"You won't get a cab to pick you up here," the attendant said. "Hell, if you was stabbed and bleeding to death, no ambulance would come here. Not at night anyway."

"Just hurry up with the van," Michael said.

The man finished the paperwork and Michael signed it, then stuffed his card and license back into his wallet.

"Here are the keys," the attendant said. "Number one-five-one."

"Where is it?" Michael asked.

"It's out there somewheres."

"Just give me some fucking idea where it is, man. Christ, you've got vans all over the place out there." Michael looked out the window. Just seeing all of the vehicles under the puddles of light made his head throb. "Look, there's three-two-seven. Let me have three-two-seven."

The man didn't want to change anything, but he scratched out the number on the form and wrote in the new one. "Okay, there you go." He handed over the papers to Michael along with a different set of keys.

Michael gave the man one last hard look.

"Just honk when you're at the gate and I'll let you out."

As they walked out to the van, Karen said, "Michael, please listen to me."

"No."

Michael unlocked the vehicle, Karen's side first. The key stuck and turned abrasively in the hole, and then they got in. "Why do they all smell like this?" he said, inserting the key into the ignition and giving it a turn. The first attempt provided nothing but a click. On the second try the engine was slow to turn over, but did. Michael gunned it a couple times, extra loud, for the benefit of the man inside who was watching them through the window. He honked at the gate, the gate opened, and they drove out onto New York Avenue.

The journey through town to Dupont Circle was tedious and uneventful. At the circle Michael drove around twice before getting on Massachusetts in the right direction. After a series of turns he managed to locate Joshua's gallery and parked the van in the circular driveway of the neighboring building. It was nearly eleven o'clock.

"You're actually going to break in?" Karen said.

"Yes. You wait here in the van."

"Michael," she complained. "What about the alarm?"

"Joshua doesn't have an alarm. He has a sign that says he has an alarm, but no alarm. He's too cheap."

"I'm scared."

"Wait here." He started to get out, then leaned back to kiss her. "Thanks for coming with me."

Michael went first to the front door and, finding it secure, he made his way along the side of the building, looking for another way in. There were three levels and Joshua lived on the top.

Michael was convinced there would be a way into the gallery. The painting was a piece of him; it had come to represent that part of himself which was still real, that part which was about the art alone, pure expression, his soul, his heart. There would be a way in. He found a window at the rear of the building that, because of its age, was loose and rattled to the touch, and he managed to work the lock open with his pocket knife. He pulled himself up and into the storage room/kitchen, being careful not to knock over the empty cartons that had been stacked haphazardly on a table beneath the window. There were spots of light throughout the rooms, lime-colored night-lights plugged into the wall outlets; an awful green, he thought, but somehow soothing to the pain in his head. He paused at the open stairway and listened for movement in the building.

Michael found the office, the same room in which he had had his last argument with Joshua. He started looking through the drawers of the file cabinet. He wanted to find any documents that pertained to his painting. He found the agreement he had signed with Joshua and burned it in the fireplace. He also burned another paper that served more or less as an inventory of the paintings delivered and the delivery manifest that listed the number of paintings.

He then went out into the gallery and saw the painting there in the dark, glowing the way he always hoped his paintings would glow in the dark. Just a few feet from it, twelve inches above the floor, was one of Joshua's hideous night-lights. Michael, with great difficulty, managed to get the painting off the wall. The canvas was not terribly heavy, but the size of it made it unwieldy. He stopped as he heard the creaking of floorboards upstairs, but the noise passed. He carried the painting to the front where he leaned the canvas against the wall of the vestibule while he unlocked and opened the door.

A gust of wind hit the canvas as he exited and took him several paces in the wrong direction, but he turned and got the edge pointed into the breeze and pushed back to the driveway where he had left Karen. The canvas was large enough that he didn't see the goings-on at the van until he was very close, although he thought he heard Karen's voice calling to him. When he could see what was going on he thought about running. Karen was leaning against the side of the van with her palms flat and her arms raised. There were two men standing with her, one going through her purse with a flashlight and another speaking on a walkie-talkie.

"What's going on?" Michael said.

"Is this your van?" the man with the walkie-talkie asked. He had an accent, Middle Eastern, Michael thought.

"Yes. And this woman is my wife."

"What is your business here?" the man asked.

"I was picking up a painting." Michael directed attention to the huge canvas he was resting on his foot.

"This is the Moroccan Embassy. You cannot park in this driveway."

"I'm sorry," Michael said. "We're done now. See, I've got the painting and we're ready to go."

"Are you an American citizen?" the man asked.

Michael nodded.

"May I see your identification?"

"May I put the painting in the van first?"

The man snapped his fingers at Karen and said, "You, wife, hold the picture."

Karen began to balk, but Michael said, "Please, honey, so we can get out of here."

Karen held the painting up while Michael produced his driver's license. The man studied it as the other man held the flashlight over his shoulder. Both men nodded, appeared satisfied, and then a blue-and-white police car pulled up and blocked the driveway. The Moroccan man with the walkie-talkie spoke into it and one of the cops spoke on his walkie-talkie and suddenly the night seemed, to Michael, to be full of static and muffled voices.

"What do we have here?" the fatter of the two fat cops asked.

"These people parked in our driveway." the man with the flashlight said. "Appears it was a mistake."

"Let me see your license," the cop said to Michael.

Michael handed it to him, since he hadn't yet put it away. The other cop walked around the van, examining it with his big flashlight.

"Okay, now turn around and put your hands against the van."

"Wait a second," Michael said.

The cop spun Michael around and pushed him against the wall of the vehicle. "Long way from home, aren't you, Mr. Lawson?" the policeman said.

"Yes, I guess I am."

"You staying around here?"

"We were in the Henley Park Hotel, but we checked out."

"Your van?"

The other cop made a complete circle around the vehicle and now stood with his partner. The two Moroccans stepped back and were quietly watching.

"No, the van is rented," Michael said.

"May I see those papers?"

"They're in my jacket pocket."

The cop reached around him, pulled the pages from his pocket, and looked them over.

"What are you doing here?" the cop asked.

"I had to get something from next door."

The cops looked over at Joshua's.

"It's a gallery," Michael said. "I had to pick up one of my paintings. This one." He pointed to the canvas with a nod. "See, it's got my name down on the corner of it. Michael Lawson. And on the back you'll find my name again and my address on a blue card."

The two fat cops talked to each other and cast a few glances at the gallery. The talking cop came back.

"It's just a little late to be picking up stuff, wouldn't you say?"

"We're headed back to Denver and it was the only time we had. The owner left the door open for me and told me to lock up. The painting has my name on it."

"It does have his name," the until-then-silent cop said.

"You guys got a problem with these people?" the first fat cop asked the two Moroccans.

"No problem."

The cop handed Michael his license, then gave the painting a good look, turning his light onto it. "You painted this, eh?"

"Yes."

"Get paid for stuff like this?"

"Yes."

"Hell, my kid could do that. Hell, he does do it." He laughed and his fat partner laughed with him as they waddled back to their patrol car.

As Michael and Karen loaded the canvas into the back of the van, the Moroccan men watched them. The one who had spoken said, "I like the picture. Nice colors. Makes me homesick." The other man nodded.

In the car, Karen was shaking. Michael studied her, feeling bad for her, hating himself for what he was putting her through. He knew he was acting like a shit, knew that she only wanted to be let in and he was taking unfair and cruel advantage, in his way laughing at her. He had all but made fun of her for being interested in the business of the art world. Why shouldn't she have been interested? Simply because he was behaving, as Joshua had pointed out, like a childish and selfish dimwit?

"I'm sorry," he said.

She looked at him.

He turned left, following the signs to the freeway. "I'm sorry for the way I've been treating you. I really love the way you're interested in what I feel, the way you're interested in my work."

She seemed moved by this.

"Thank you for coming with me."

She looked forward out the window.

"Do you think I'm crazy?" Michael asked, merging into the fast-moving traffic.

"No," she said.

"Tell the truth."

"No."

Michael decided then, that in some way, probably not a significant or pivotal way, Karen was not to be trusted—that her judgment was at best suspect or that she was simply a liar. Whether she was seeking to protect him or not, it didn't much matter.

PERCIVAL EVERETT is the author of eight books, among them *God's Country* and *Zulus*. He lives with his wife on a farm in Southern California and is a professor of creative writing at the University of California, Riverside.

This book was designed by Will Powers. It is set in Galliard and Modula Serif type by Stanton Publications Services, Inc. and manufactured by BookCrafters on acid-free paper. Cover design by Ann Artz.